LP
FIC
WHE

38749007800327

Wheeler, Richard S
author.
Easy pickings

W9-ASR-650

Hickory Flat Public Library
2740 East Cherokee Drive
Canton, Georgia 30115

SEQUOYAH REGIONAL LIBRARY

3 8749 0078 00327

EASY PICKINGS

Center Point
Large Print

Also by Richard S. Wheeler and available from
Center Point Large Print:

The Two Medicine River
Richard Lamb
The Fate
East Street
Anything Goes
Brass in the Desert

**This Large Print Book carries the
Seal of Approval of N.A.V.H.**

EASY PICKINGS

Richard S. Wheeler

CENTER POINT LARGE PRINT
THORNDIKE, MAINE

PROPERTY OF
SEQUOYAH REGIONAL
LIBRARY SYSTEM

This Center Point Large Print edition
is published in the year 2016 by arrangement with
St. Martin's Press.

Copyright © 2016 by Richard S. Wheeler.

All rights reserved.

This is a work of fiction.
All of the characters, organizations, and events portrayed
in this novel are either products of the author's
imagination or are used fictitiously.

The text of this Large Print edition is unabridged.
In other aspects, this book may vary
from the original edition.
Printed in the United States of America
on permanent paper.
Set in 16-point Times New Roman type.

ISBN: 978-1-68324-179-9

Library of Congress Cataloging-in-Publication Data

Names: Wheeler, Richard S., author.
Title: Easy pickings / Richard S. Wheeler.
Description: Center Point Large Print edition. | Thorndike, Maine :
Center Point Large Print, 2016.
Identifiers: LCCN 2016034405 | ISBN 9781683241799
    (hardcover : alk. paper)
Subjects: LCSH: Gold mines and mining—Fiction. | Widows—Fiction. |
Large type books. | GSAFD: Western stories.
Classification: LCC PS3573.H4345 E165 2016 | DDC 813/.54—dc23
LC record available at https://lccn.loc.gov/2016034405

To my resourceful and courageous friend
Margot Kidder

EASY PICKINGS

ONE

Kermit was dead. A slab of rock had dropped from the top and flattened him.

March stared at her man, terrified that more lethal rock would fall from the roof of the shaft and kill her, too. She backed out, into daylight, her heart racing, glad to have the sun above her and not sinister rock.

He had not shown up for his noon porridge. That meant he was feverishly excavating a new pocket, or was dead. She had left Fourth, their boy, alone and hiked up the grade and shouted into the mine tunnel, which bore into a steep slope. There had been only silence.

She shouted, again, and was met with a foreboding quiet.

She had edged in, afraid and angry, and found him fifty feet back, under a gray tombstone that had caught him squarely and crushed life from him. His flattened head was visible, along with a twisted arm.

Horrified, she stood before the mine shaft, staring down a vast pine-clad slope to the creek and the trail that would take her to town for help.

"Kermit. Talk to me, please, please."

But she knew he wouldn't.

The damned fool, she thought, and then relented.

Kermit McPhee the Third was a stubborn man, and had said he would put up timbering when he was good and ready, and for now, he wasn't ready. March had been just as stubborn, foreseeing this, and they had been at loggerheads for weeks about it. A wave of tenderness caught her. Kermit McPhee was the man she had crushed to her chest, the man who had gotten her with child, a little one they called Fourth because he was the fourth Kermit McPhee. Now she was a widow with a gold mine.

She fled down the rocky path to the log cabin that had been their mountain refuge for almost a year, the place where they huddled against Montana blizzards and winds. Fourth dozed in sunlight that filtered through the sole window. She would need to go to town. The slab was too heavy for her to lift from Kermit. She would need to free him and bury him. And then what?

She wasn't ready to go to town. She felt the shock steal strength from her limbs. She sagged onto a chair at the rough table, and sat there, paralyzed. She had been named after the stormiest month in Scotland, and she had given him a stormy marriage. He knew she would when he had asked her. He had wanted that. There was nothing placid about Kermit McPhee the Third. Now she was angry with him. He had put off timbering. She had nagged him, and that had only made him more stubborn about it.

The mine penetrated only a hundred feet or so, the shaft rising slightly. He was always working in the light flooding in from its portal, and that had betrayed him. He was working a good quartz seam, and once a week or so he had loaded the mule with gold ore and taken it to Marysville, where there was an assayer who also bought small lots of ore.

"I'll put in timbers when I'm good and ready," he had said. "Powder and fuse, tools, drills, they're robbing me blind."

He had a point. They barely scraped by, and only because she sewed his rags together and bought the cheapest cereals, and patched her gowns and resisted her yearnings for a few comforts.

She left the memory alone and threw a shawl around her shoulders. The walk to Marysville would take half an hour, and the air was sharp. She swaddled Fourth in a blanket and set out, down the long trail through pine woods and over rocky shoulders, until she reached the gulch that would snake its way into town.

She didn't know who to tell, what to ask, what to say, but it would not matter. Fourth would be cared for, somehow. Marysville was a company town in a mountain-girt basin, existing to support Thomas Cruse's giant Drumlummon Mine and reduction works on the other side of the valley. It brimmed with cottages and pubs, dry goods stores and groceries. She thought that the town had a constable, but she wasn't sure she needed one. She needed someone to free Kermit and bury him. Marysville was the most peaceful place she had ever seen. Hardly anyone died in Marysville except careless miners, and she wasn't sure whether it had an undertaker, or much of a cemetery. Or whether she could bury a Scot in one.

The closer she came to town, the deeper her loss. At first she was mad at Kermit and then sickened, but now she knew she would miss him, especially when he would sip a little single malt and sing bawdy ballads to her. She was grateful that Fourth was too young to understand them, but they made the baby laugh because the Third laughed.

She passed the outlying cottages, some with rambling roses and picket fences, and made her way into the heart of town, closer to the giant works of the Cruse mine. She knew the assayer there, Mr. Wittgenstein, and thought to ask him for two men. It'd take two to release Kermit and get him onto a pallet.

But then she spotted the mortuary. Laidlow's Funeral Home. Of course. She had forgotten about Mortimer Laidlow. She had been more interested in life than death. But now she needed his help.

But it wasn't a man who greeted her. It was a voluptuous young woman, with sleek brown hair and a lot of frippery sewn to her green dress. That kind of woman shouldn't work in a funeral parlor.

"Never mind," March said.

"Mr. Laidlow's in Helena today, ma'am."

"I'll get some miners," March said.

"You've lost someone. Let me help you."

Fourth was squirming. March suspected the diapers needed changing. She had none with her.

"You are?"

"I'm Mistletoe. Mr. Laidlow uses me when he has need. We want to share your grief, carry your burdens, lighten your load," the girl said.

"Here," March said, and thrust Fourth at the woman.

Fourth squirmed, and a stink smote the air. Gingerly, the girl in green frippery accepted the baby. She was not familiar with babies.

"Mining accident. My man's dead, rock on his head. Send two men with some equipment to get the rock off, and then we'll put him in the graveyard."

"I'd better wait for Mr. Laidlow, madam."

"Never mind, I'll get help."

March collected Fourth and started out.

"Give me a name and a place, and I'll send a wagon up," the young lady said. "We're here to help you in your time of grief."

March did. Even drew a little map.

March wasn't sure she was grieving properly. Kermit had been stubborn, and she was stubborn, and the log cabin half up a mountain wasn't her idea of a good life.

"Do you have a diaper, by any chance?" she asked.

"We have everything but diapers here, Mrs. McPhee. Now while you're here, you might want to look at coffins. They are a way of honoring the departed."

"Cheapest on your shelf. Pine box. That's how Kermit would want it. He begrudged a spare farthing."

"And you might want to look at headstones."

"I have dripping diapers and you talk headstones."

She retreated into sunlight.

Mistletoe might or might not send help. March headed for the assayer, Mr. Wittgenstein, bald with wire-rimmed glasses guarding baggy eyes, and found him studying a bead of gold in a ceramic dish.

"You, is it, Mrs. McPhee?"

"Kermit Three is lying under a rock and I need two men to get him out."

"Is it urgent?"

"He's dead, and I don't want rats eating him."

"You need a diaper. The miasma of a diaper fouls my chemistry." He looked around. "Over there. The dish towel."

"That's the first kind thing anyone's said to me, Mr. Wittgenstein."

She settled Fourth on a specimen table and set to work. "The girl at the funeral home said she'd send some men, but I doubt it. Would you send some men, with equipment?"

"Consider it done. I'll go. I know how to get there."

Indeed, the assayer had visited Kermit's gold mine several times.

March changed the diaper and rinsed the used one in a zinc sink.

"It'll be an hour," the assayer said. "I'll take the afternoon off."

March lifted Kermit Four and headed into fresh air. Assay offices stank of chemicals. She preferred the smell of dirty diapers. There was nothing left to do in town, so she started back to the McPhee. Kermit Three had named it after himself, which irked her. A more gallant man would have called it the March Mine. Usually, a man named a mine after his sweetheart. If Mr. Laidlow got himself a mine, he probably would name the shaft after Mistletoe.

She dreaded the long climb that would take her to the horror hidden in a hollow in a fir-clad slope. But ere long she discovered a wagon closing behind her, with two burly youths urging a dray along. They drew up and halted.

"Climb in, madam," said the carrot-haired one. They were young men, not boys.

She hesitated.

"Mr. Laidlow's assistant sent us," the man said. "I'm Jerusalem."

"I will, Mr. Jerusalem," she said.

"No, that's my first name. Jerusalem Jones. This is Bum Carp. Mr. Laidlow's our uncle, and we do odd jobs."

They made room for her on the seat, while eyeing Fourth as if he were a meteor.

The dray dragged the creaky wagon upward, along a defile, over a tumbling rivulet, past the first larkspur, and finally into a chill, silent world scarcely imagined by those in town.

The two rescuers stepped down uneasily, staring at the small aperture in the gray rock and the skittery rails that erupted like writhing snakes out of the cliff. There wasn't much to see. No mine works, no towering heaps of tailings.

The sun lay low now, throwing the cliff into shadow, so that the shaft formed a black square mouth against cold rock. The height of the shaft was barely six feet, so low that the cruel rock lowered upon anyone who braved the confines of that little tunnel.

The pair stared.

"You want us to go in there?"

"He's back a ways."

"I don't like it," Bum said.

She didn't blame him. Especially after a slab of stone had murdered her man. But sometimes things needed doing.

"Follow me," she said, setting Fourth on the stony ground. She pushed in, felt the damp close air, edged back, while the pair watched. Then she stopped. Kermit lay there, under that burden, his face as gray as the rock.

"Well?" she asked.

"I think you should leave him there," said Jerusalem. "Seal it off."

The two glanced at each other.

She sensed that these two would not bring her man out. She retreated from the darkness. The shaft was so low in places she herself could barely stand up in it.

"Not much of a mine anyway," Jerusalem said.

"It is all I have," she said.

"Never got you much," he said. "Or maybe that's a bad guess."

"I will take a pry bar in and lift one side. I will have you slide him out," she said.

"That's too much for you, and dangerous. This shaft should be timbered," he said.

She found the long pry bar, spaded at one end, and walked in. She could find no way to slide the bar past her man and lift up.

"You, Bum, you come lift the rock. I'll slide my man out from under."

"I'd risk my neck going into there."

"My man went in every day, all day, digging quartz."

"And look at him now, ma'am."

She felt a rush of anger. "Come with me and lift. I'll do the rest."

But the pair shuffled uneasily, their minds hardening against the thing that needed doing.

They weren't experienced miners, not used to darkness and close quarters and rock everywhere. And they would not go where Kermit went every day. She sensed they had been in a few mines, and were afraid of this one.

She found some wooden blocks that Kermit used in his work, and hauled them in. They watched her from safe daylight. She took the pry bar in the fading light and gently worked it past the body of her man, and lifted. The brutal rock came grudgingly. When she could lift no more, she pushed a block under the bar, let it down, and rested. She did it again, pushing the block farther. Then she tugged gently at the shoulders of her man, and he scraped toward her. She pulled again, and then he was free, and she dragged him, a foot at a time, toward light.

While the two young men watched, cowards that they were.

TWO

She stared down at the crushed gray flesh of the man she had held so tight in her arms, and felt drained. Something good and true had gone away.

The two men stared, and then glanced at the mine.

"Help me carry him down to the cabin," she said.

"It's kind of a nice place you have here," Jerusalem Jones allowed.

Neither of them moved.

"I will go get a winding sheet," she said, and headed wearily down the rocky path. The two young men were useless. She took Fourth with her. He nestled on her hip and clung as she descended. She settled him in his crib, pulled a sheet off the bed, and carried it up the slope where the men stood.

She spread the sheet over the rocky ground, and then rolled Kermit into it, and then she wrapped him in it, taking one last look at his broken face.

"There," she said, rising, waiting for the young men. "You can take him to the wagon."

"I guess you're gonna sell the gold mine," Jerusalem said.

So that was what this was about.

She spotted Rolf Wittgenstein laboring up the

trail, and noted that he had changed his clothing. He wore a dark suit now, with a cravat.

"Ah, Mrs. McPhee, I see these young men have freed your husband. Very courageous of them. I came to offer help, if help be needed."

"I did it."

"Well, these two can help carry the deceased to Mr. Laidlow's wagon."

"I would prefer that you and I do it, Mr. Wittgenstein."

He stared, an eyebrow arching above his wire-rimmed glasses.

"It shall be our sad duty, then."

Some blood had leaked onto the sheet, but the assayer didn't hesitate to pick up Kermit by his shoulders, while she clasped his feet. Together, and slowly, they made their way down the rocky path. Kermit seemed feather light, as if all his weight had been in the breath of life. The young men lingered at the mine head, and did not follow behind.

She caught a glimpse of them peering into the mine, and studying the works, including the sole ore car, the rails, a pile of crossties, a box of caps, and a coil of fuse, and especially stray pieces of white quartz that lay about. Jerusalem pocketed several of the glistening pieces.

Then they were out of sight. She and the assayer descended steadily, not speaking until they reached the black wagon and gently laid Kermit in it and arranged the sheet to cover the dead properly.

"He was a good and hardworking man, your husband," he said, as if to fill a need to say something uplifting.

"They wouldn't go in and get him. They're Laidlow nephews supposedly helping out. But they wouldn't do it, and now they're hanging about up there. It's not hard to see what they are thinking. I mean the mine, here for the taking."

"It would be easy to do," he said. "That's it, I suppose. You will want to get help."

"They will learn that March is a mean month where we come from."

"I suppose I could drive this wagon down to Marysville," he said.

"I would like you to stay for the moment. I don't wish to be left alone with those two."

"Yes, that's a good point. They are obvious, aren't they?"

"The federal patent's in the cabin. We proved it up."

"It would be well not to tell them anything at all."

"I wasn't planning to."

Fourth stirred in his crib and whimpered. The child had been quiet through all this turmoil, but now he was sensing that his small world was falling away.

"Tea, Mr. Wittgenstein?"

"That would take a lot of doing," he said, eyeing her cold stove. "If you will forgive me, madam, this mine needs protecting. Your husband was barely lost to you before the vultures began to circle. And it's only beginning. They will find ways to drive you off. They will try to scare you, bully you, deceive you, get you to sell for little or nothing. Or even worse."

She smiled wanly. "So I've heard. Propose marriage. Find ways to steal the mine. Abduct this child. These things are churning in me, and we haven't even gotten my husband buried."

"They will come to me, wanting to know about the ore," he said. There was a question in it.

"It's no secret. Kermit delighted in telling the world. The farther in he goes, the better it gets, and there is no lateral limit discovered so far. That little shaft pierces a lode that runs to either side, but no one knows how much."

Wittgenstein rubbed his bald head. "For the time being, madam, if anyone inquires about the values in the ore, I will decline to answer. If you should sell the mine, you would want me to supply figures to your buyer."

March felt a wave of weariness. "Please drive him down the road. I don't think they'll bother me."

"I would not think of leaving you, in such circumstances, Mrs. McPhee. I shall bide my time here at the wagon."

She nodded, thinking she ought to make him

some tea. But instead, she slipped inside and collapsed in a Morris chair that had been Kermit's pride. She sensed his presence there, in that chair, and it comforted her. The things that gold did to people had not surprised her.

Shortly, the young men swung into the yard, having explored the works to their hearts' content. She heard the assayer talking to them. Then one of them, Jerusalem Jones, barged into her cabin without knocking.

"We'll keep an eye on it for you," he said.

"That will not be necessary."

"There's people wanting this mine, and we'll be keeping an eye out for you."

"The mine, Mr. Jones, is no one's business but my own."

He grinned. "You've gotta keep people out of it."

Wearily she watched him clamber into the wagon, beside her dead man, while the other man slapped lines over the rump of the dray, and they rattled away, and then the widow and son of Kermit McPhee were engulfed in quietness, and twilight crept along the slopes.

"I will be going now, Mrs. McPhee. Unless there is need."

"Thank you for coming, Mr. Wittgenstein. I want to be alone now."

She watched him walk down the grade, a little way behind the youths and their wagon.

She felt numb. She had dwelled in an isolated

cabin, had no friends in town, and her life had been bounded by husband and son. There would be no friends collecting here to comfort her and see to her needs. The cabin was a comfort now, and so was the privacy.

She lay still, too weary even to brew some tea. Soon she would need to feed Fourth and herself, too, if she felt hungry. She hadn't the faintest idea where her life would lead now. Marriage? She'd had her fill of it. And soon the pressure would begin. There were men itching to marry a young widow with a working gold mine. She had no desire for them, no wish to accommodate them. Kermit the Third was enough.

The cabin didn't seem empty; Kermit's presence lingered there. He had actually devoted time to civilizing the place, building their tables and chairs, putting up shelves, getting up a fine out-house that was not icy in winter. The cabin was not a hard place to be, even though it was a long walk from company, a half hour from groceries and meat markets and dry goods stores and saloons and blacksmiths. Sometimes in the winter they had been cut off, and only then was she uneasy and aching to be reconnected.

The child was restless. She bestirred herself, built a small fire, jacked some water from the shallow well, and started it heating. She would cook some porridge for the boy and herself later, and get some tea going.

The men would be down to Marysville by now, and she knew that the assayer would insist that they go first to Laidlow's place and carry Kermit McPhee in. She didn't know how she would pay for all that. The mine hadn't made them rich. But she would somehow. Mr. Wittgenstein would see to her needs. He was a strange man, pale, bald, and not an outdoor sort of male, and yet scrupulous in his dealings. Today she saw him quite stern, his hard gaze compelling those renegade young men to do what was right and needful, even if they were busy scheming.

After waiting for the porridge to cool, she fed Fourth, cleaned him, and slipped him into his cradle. The poor baby would never know his father. She eyed him gently as she pulled her hand-crocheted coverlet over him and blew out the lamp.

Death, then. She sagged into a chair, scarcely knowing what would come next. A stiff breeze rattled the shutters that guarded the sole window. She felt too alone. Had she known people in Marysville, there would be friends here, a quiet vigil beside a young widow. Mining towns saw many vigils, not only for men lost in the bowels of the earth, but men lost in the cruel milling machinery that crushed and refined and smelted ore, eating up cordwood and an occasional mortal as well. Mining was a cruel business. The earth exacted its toll of lives and property.

This was one of few times she had spent a night alone, with Kermit gone, and it amplified every sound that the night brought on the breeze. She swore she heard footsteps, but cast the idea aside. She was overwrought. Still, the grate of boot on gravel continued. It was as if several men were passing the darkened cottage in the night, heading for the mine for whatever reason.

But there were no voices. And no other night sounds. And for a while all she sensed was the deep silence of her cabin. Its thick logs had once seemed stout, but somehow just now they seemed frail, as if some terrible force could turn her refuge into matchsticks.

She could not say why she sensed something was wrong. Nor could she say why she wrapped a shawl about her against the chill, and stepped into the night, and slowly, cautiously made her way up the rocky trail to the mine, starting at every slight sound. She dreaded leaving Fourth alone in his crib, dreaded the foolishness that was propelling her upward toward the mine, only a few hours after the terrible accident that had killed Kermit.

She scolded herself. What sort of foolishness would drive her, and what did she expect to see? She climbed slowly, the familiar trail a comfort to her. She had passed up and down a thousand times, and knew every pebble. She arrived at the rocky ledge where the mine pierced into the bowels of the mountain, and knew at once that something wasn't right, but in the stygian gloom she could make out nothing. She heard, rather than saw, that mortals were there, and they were busy, and muttering things among themselves.

She thought to stop them, but knew better, and knew that her safety depended on the darkness enveloping her. She stepped off the trail, straining to grasp what was happening, knowing only from the soft growl of human voices that something was occurring there.

She heard the hard sound of running, boots clattering on gravel, and several of these night visitors raced by, some of them only twenty or thirty feet from where she stood beside a jagged rock that had split from the bedrock beside the road.

A dull thump slammed her, along with a muted flash and then the sound of clattering rock. A wave of cordite smoke smote her. It didn't last. A breeze whipped the air clean, and the debris settled into silence. She stood, paralyzed, uncertain what had happened. No one remained, as far as she could tell, but she didn't dare move. So she stood, her nerves screaming, her muscles taut, and finally when she could endure it no more she edged upward, seeing no one, her eyes upon a slope revealed only by bright stars, somehow changed.

She stumbled over shattered rock, and realized that the whole ledge above the portal of the mine lay under debris, and she would need to poke and probe her way up to the mine head, which she did with care and fear.

The mine had disappeared. Rather, the shaft lay under a mountain of rubble, sealed from the world. She could see no ore car. She thought she might see rails dimly reflecting the night, but she saw no rails. She saw no powder magazine, no cordwood, nothing but an anonymous slope where once a small mine shaft had pierced horizontally into the mountain. Kermit's gold mine had ceased to exist. For the moment, anyway.

She choked back a cry, aware that there might be observers still, observers who would not be present to comfort a widow on the very night of her husband's death. She stared, amazed and afraid, the anger building in her.

And then she smelled smoke, and caught the flicker of flame. She stumbled down the trail, her heart in her throat, hoping to reach her burning cabin before it was too late.

THREE

She rounded a bend in the flickering light and beheld her cabin engulfed in fierce flames. A wall of yellow barred the door. A wall of yellow barred the window. A roar echoed up the gulch. She raced toward the inferno, her heart hammering.

"Fourth," she cried, and plunged toward the door, but the heat rebuffed her, threw her back, singed her hair and scorched her robe. She ran around the cabin, looking for some way in, but there was none. The cabin roared and seethed and spat tongues of blinding flame. She heard a cry, clear and plaintive, over the roar.

The smell of kerosene hung in the air. Light danced off the nearby forest. Smoke eddied down, after boiling upward. Thunderous flame blistered her, drove her back, and finally pushed her to the earth. Sparks shot high, and embers sailed into the night and fell about her.

She ached for her baby. She cried out to him. She itched to plunge through the flame, get inside, and snatch him out. Maybe the well would help. She raced to the pump handle and began cranking it, finally getting a little water, and then more. But she had no pail. She pulled off her robe and soaked it, and soaked herself, and put the wet robe on, and splashed water into her hair, and braved the heat, but the wet robe and wet hair were nothing, and the heat threw her back and murdered hope.

Then she lay on the sod, broken and numb, knowing all there was to know, and hoping that the infant was gone before flame licked his soft little body. But that was something she would never know.

She sat numbly while the cabin burnt to the ground and became a glowing orange heap throwing vicious heat at her. She thought of nothing, the mesmerizing fire blotting out every-thing. Smoke lowered, and so did the first chill, and she saw stars again, and knew she had to move, because the night was cold. She was a half hour from anywhere, in a damp robe and slippers, and had nothing else. Everything she had ever owned or known was gone.

She sat paralyzed until night stabbed at her, and she knew she must walk to Marysville, must get help, must tell someone that on this night vandals had come and taken everything from her. Her life was smoke.

The heat had mostly dried her robe. That was the sole comfort that March McPhee possessed. She did not know the time. She didn't know if she could make it to Marysville in her robe and slippers. But she started, not wanting to leave her baby, still hoping to hear his little cry in the middle of the ashes. But she walked, feeling sticks and stones push upon her slippers, walking down the steep trail that divided the gulch. She walked, and rested, and walked, and the stars moved in their nightly orbits, and she walked more, as the heavens whirled.

She felt out of her body. She could not connect herself to her own flesh, her own muscle. She seemed to float, disembodied, as the gulch twisted lower and finally opened on a dark flat, where Marysville lay silent, its lamps out. No light rose anywhere save the Drumlummon works on the far slope and the mill works below it, where getting gold from rock never ceased.

She looked for a lamp. She saw only dark frame buildings, black against the sky. She needed a lamp, a person, but the mining town slumbered. She hated the place. Those who had killed her baby were here. Those who had blown apart the mine to keep others out of it had come from this place.

It was very late. The saloons were done. The constable was in bed, wherever he lived.

She thought of Laidlow's Funeral Home, but something stayed her. The hooligans that had come from there were probably the hooligans who had just robbed her of her baby. She stood wearily, so worn she didn't know what to do. A quarter moon had risen.

"Well, missy, you seem to be in a fix," a quiet voice said.

She whirled, and found a stout, balding, jowly man staring at her.

"I need help."

"That's for sure, madam. Is there no one looking after you?"

"I lost everything. The fire . . ."

"A fire was it?"

"Far from here. Up our gulch."

"If you're willing, come with me. I just closed my saloon. I had a gent stay on, talking of his woes, and he wouldn't quit, and that's what a saloon man is for, the listening. But I'll open up. Or, take you to wherever you're going."

It was a question.

She had never been in a saloon. But she nodded.

He led her a half a block to a dark building with locked double doors.

"Or we can wake up the constable," he said.

"Let me talk."

He unlocked, pushed open the door, and she entered into a dark world, rank with strange odors: cigars, whiskey, sweat.

"I am Tipperary Leary," he said. "I've heard a lot of stories in my day."

She didn't want to say her name.

He struck a match and lit a kerosene lamp, and now she saw she was in a long, narrow place, with a bar running along most of the right wall. There were some tables and chairs dimly visible at the rear. In the dull light she saw horse art on the walls, fancy nags drawing carriages.

He eyed her quietly. "Have a seat, madam, and I'll get you some water. Unless you need something else."

"Water," she said.

He handed her a glass filled with cool water, and waited.

"I'm listening," he said. "That is, if you've a story. Maybe it's not one to be told to a stranger."

In truth, she was trying to sort out what to say. She didn't know this man. He could be one of them, one of the ones who . . . She caught herself. "It's not a long story, sir."

He found a bowl of pretzels and placed it before her, and drew some beer from a tap and then sat across a scarred table from her.

She was right. It didn't take much telling. He sat quietly, sipping, listening, not missing anything, saying anything.

And then she was done.

"You've lost more this day than most lose in a lifetime, madam," he said. "It's a wonder you're here and telling it."

She was aware that she had yet to speak her name.

"And here you are, in a robe, and needing help, and I'm not the man to put you in proper clothing, having none, and I have but a small room in a boarding house. But I can make a few things happen. First, though, have you the need to report it? We have a constable."

"I don't know what I want. Tell someone, I guess."

He eyed her quietly. "I'd not want anything, either. I'd want to crawl into a bed and stay there. And ache for those I lost."

She didn't respond.

"I'll be doing some things for you, then," he said. "First, if you'd like a little bite, there's hard-boiled eggs in that jar, and pickles, there, and pretzels. A little something for the stomach. And anything else here . . ."

She nodded.

"Now I'm going to be leaving you for a bit. I know where to get you some clothing. You haven't a thing but what's on your back. You'll not want to know how I'll get it, but it's all that can be done at this hour. I'll want your slipper, for size, and I'll want you to tell me the rest, for fitting."

"Medium and . . . oh, say I'm stocky. And not gaudy. I can't pay. . . ."

"I'm owed for some favors, and don't you worry about a thing."

He vanished into the depths of night. She sat, desolately, and then fancied a pretzel, and nibbled on it absently. She needed to make some decisions—but was too numb to think, and finally slumped in her chair, quietly, growing aware that time was slipping away.

She knew there were a couple of public women in town. Mining towns were like that. She had given them absolutely no thought, nor did she really know what drove men to them. Was it the same as what drove Kermit to her?

She wanted only to sleep and not wake up. The saloon was cold, but her robe shielded her from the worst of it. She lost track of time, and then she heard him again. He had some things neatly folded, and he nodded to her.

"There's a closet," he said, carrying the lamp to a rear door.

Minutes later she emerged wearing a plain and shapeless blue dress and soft doeskin slippers.

"Mr. Leary," she said. "You've been good to me."

"Thank Molly," he replied. " 'Twas nothing. She didn't mind helping."

"I can manage now."

"And where would that be taking you?"

She didn't know. Back into the night.

"I've been thinking a bit, Mrs.— Did you say a name?"

"McPhee. March McPhee. My husband was Kermit."

"You know, sometimes dark deeds start a man thinking, and I've been doing that, running about

Marysville in the wee hours. I think you might be hasty, making your troubles known entire. You've got some gold-fevered rotters stealing your mine and killing you and your child, men who might strike again if they knew you were alive. And I don't see that the constable could help you any, with nothing to go on. He's a fine old gent, with gray whiskers and a nightstick, and he's very good at boxing the ears of little boys when they torment dogs. I imagine he even knows which end of a revolver is the muzzle.

"But as I am saying, I'm not good with words, you don't know who the devils might be, and a gold mine is a prize big enough to forget their ordinary decency, and do whatever needs doing to grab the mine away. I'm thinking for your safety, you might want to take a little different road, and if you should, you can count on my help. I'd take it as an honor."

"I don't know. I want to bury Kermit. I want to bury my baby. I want to send them to heaven—if there is any. I struggle with those things. But I don't struggle with doing what's right and proper. A place of rest, a prayer over his grave. A farewell to one I made my own. Some respect. Just a little respect."

"There will be good time for that; it doesn't matter if this is tomorrow or a week or a month. And the grieving won't change."

"I can't make these decisions, Mr. Leary. I can

hardly remember my name, or Kermit's name, or the baby's name."

"Whatever you wish, it's my honor to help you get there. I'd say you've got several candidates wanting your mine. One is the assayer, Wittgenstein. Another is those two brutes who studied you and the mine and offered a new widow no help. Another is the young woman at the funeral home who sent them. Another is Laidlow himself, though you didn't meet him there. She might have told him plenty. Who knows who else, eh? Some or several of them want the mine, and would strike again."

"Not the assayer. A gentleman if ever there was. My husband dealt with him month after month, and Kermit had only good to say of him."

"Forgive me, Mrs. McPhee, but he's a man who knew more about that mine, and the ore that kept getting better and better, than anyone else."

"It's not in him, Mr. Leary. He it was who helped me carry Kermit down from the mine."

Leary shrugged. "I am at your service, whatever you choose. And if you lack a shelter, there's the billiard table, got in here just a fortnight ago from St. Louis, and it'll make you a proper bed for the rest of the night."

He stood quietly, awaiting her decision.

"Mr. Leary, what you say makes sense, but I am tired and sick at heart and need a little nap. Could I wait until morning?"

He nodded. Somehow he produced a heavy coat for a pillow, and a carriage robe for a blanket.

"I'll be by when it's well into daylight, and I'll be thinking of the two whose souls have started their long walk across the skies," he said.

She watched him lumber toward the front door. Moments later, she snuffed the lamp and crawled onto the hardest bed she had ever known.

FOUR

March thought she hadn't slept. She was aware only of lying on a cruel surface, aching for her baby. But after a moment's confusion, she remembered she was in a saloon, and a kind man had given her shelter.

She sat up suddenly. Daylight puddled below a grimy window. Then she saw him, unmoving behind the bar.

He noticed.

"I thought to be watching over you," he said.

He looked different in daylight, a little younger perhaps.

She realized he had quietly spent the rest of that terrible night there, behind his bar. A great tenderness coiled up in her. "I feel safe," she said. "Thank you."

"I'll be stepping out while you look after your needs," he said. "Then we'll see what the day brings."

He left his stool and headed through the door, blinding her with momentary sunlight in that shadowed place.

After she had wearily washed her face and looked after herself, she headed for the street door and nodded him in.

"I'm all yours to command," he said. "Have you given matters some thought?"

She hadn't, and yet she knew what she would do.

"I want to arrange a service for my husband and baby. I want to bury them. So yes, I want to go to Laidlow's and talk to the man."

"Then we'll do it," he said. But then paused. "If you want me along."

"I do," she said.

"There may be those at that place who would not welcome the sight of a witness, an heir to the mine, and a survivor of an attempt to kill her."

"I have a husband, and I have a little boy, and they need to be laid to rest, sir."

"Then I'll be helping you do it, if you want the help."

"I'd be thankful. I can barely make myself think. Some day, I'll repay you."

"Repay me? Surely you don't think it's owed."

She owed him. She would repay someday. But she wouldn't argue it with him. He poured some tea, and added some crumpets he had gotten somewhere in Marysville.

"I left a wife in County Clare, coming here for the mines, but then she died of the lung sickness," he said. "Gold takes us away from our own."

"I came with Kermit," she said. "And spent my days fighting catarrh and keeping us warm. This is a cold place."

"Yes, and there's no comfort when gold's lying about, waiting to be fought over."

They pushed into sharp air, and walked to Laidlow's whitewashed funeral home, which slumbered in the early light. The town shimmered in the breeze.

A pullcord rang a bell that summoned the proprietor. The owner took his time, perhaps not used to responding at an unusual hour.

But at last a gent in muttonchops and a black frock coat opened, and eyed them.

"You must be Mrs. McPhee," he said. "Do come in. We've been awaiting you."

She nodded, and they entered. The mortician steered them to a small office, his gaze questioning Tip Leary.

"Now then, your bereavement is a matter of deepest concern for me. I want to do whatever is possible to accommodate you in your hour of need."

She let him drone on a little. He was describing his services, and raising questions.

"There'll be a service for another," she said. "The baby, Kermit the Fourth. He died in the fire."

"Fire?"

"Our cabin was burned."

Laidlow seemed puzzled enough. She talked of the fire. She didn't talk of the sealing of the mine, or her absence from the cabin. He listened intently. She saw no sign of the young woman who was keeping the doors open the previous day.

"You will need to comb the ash to find my baby. If there's anything left. McPhees burn as fast as any other mortal."

Laidlow fussed a little with some wire-rimmed spectacles. "Have you reported this, madam?"

"That will come. Now, you find my baby. I couldn't even get close in the night, it was so hot."

"We may not be able to, madam."

"You mean there'll be nothing left. Not so much as a lock of his hair as a keepsake."

"I will send some assistants. Young men I employ. This is grievous for you. And if we find the child . . ."

"Cremate him. If he is not yet ash, let him be ash. It is the only dignity."

"Now there is the matter of a coffin, and a grave, or two graves, and a service, Mrs. McPhee. And knowing how much you wish to honor your loved ones, I think a good stone would be appropriate, with the names of both incised upon it. Of course, with your considerable assets, you need not worry about managing the obligations. There are some fine lots at the front of the cemetery, a few dollars more but you need not walk to the pauper's field at the rear whenever you wish to spend a quiet hour with your loved ones."

And so it went. March grew weary of the negotiations, but in due course they set a day, the following Thursday; a place, a chapel; and a coffin, a pine box stained to look like hickory.

"And where may we find you, Mrs. McPhee?"

"At the mine," she said.

"And you have means, of course. I believe the total will be two hundred and forty."

"In time," she said.

"I will send along a little agreement," he said. "You'll need to sign it for us to proceed."

Leary had said not a word, but had absorbed it all, and when they reached fresh air, she asked him what he thought.

"You are a courageous woman, March McPhee. I don't know where you'll be staying at the mine, at the place where everything burnt to ash, but at least you'll see who the man sends to look for your baby—and maybe you'll be seeing the very ones that snuffed the life of that bright boy, the very ones who'll comb the ash for whatever's left of the boy."

"Where's the constable, Mr. Leary?"

"Would you like me to come?"

"You are my help."

He led her to a small whitewashed structure that was at once Marysville's city hall and peace officer's quarters. The little town was stirring at last, with shoppers out on the streets and deliverymen stocking stores. Leary opened for her, and she discovered a wiry mustachioed man in a blue serge suit, the sole occupant.

"Constable Roach, may I present a fine lady, Mrs. McPhee. There's been a bit of trouble."

"Trouble, eh? What sort of trouble? Have a seat, madam. And you, if you want," Roach said, nodding at a stool.

She poured her story into the silence, starting with the cave-in, quest for help, the pair sent by the funeral parlor, and later, that night, the thump, the fire, the loss.

Roach listened intently, rheumy brown eyes assessing her in a way that made her feel as if she were not the victim, but the suspect.

"Gold mine, was it?" he asked. "I think I know the one."

She saw where his thoughts were running.

"And what is this gent's role in all this?"

"Mr. Leary offered help when I arrived deep in the night and didn't know how to locate you or get help."

Roach eyed Leary with the same assessing gaze, adding to his list of suspects. But then he surprised her. "My powers extend only to city limits. That's a matter for the sheriff, up there. But I think the fire was likely an accident. You were a bit distraught, weren't you? Losing your source of income. I'd hardly call it arson, much less manslaughter. It doesn't take much. Leave a lamp burning, did you?"

She fought back the impulse to shout at him. The mine was sealed with an explosion. The cabin was doused in kerosene. An obvious attempt to kill a surviving heir to Kermit McPhee's property.

She glanced at Leary, who sat on the stool with compressed lips. Somehow she could read Leary's thoughts, and he was warning her to back away, fast, hard.

"Those people at Laidlow's. Fine fellows, and that young lady's a niece of mine, Mistletoe Harp, a bit flighty but otherwise just fine," Roach said. "Those boys, they're my nephews, Jones and Carp. I can't say I'm proud of them, not wanting to go in there to help free your husband. But boys are scaredy-cats, and I guess you showed 'em a thing or two. They just need some weathering."

That's all it took. March felt as alone in the world as a mortal can be.

"That mine's not worth a plugged nickel anyway, so I hear, so there's no cause for anyone to cop it. Whoever planted the charge did you a favor," Roach said. "Pocket mine. Clean out a ledge and quit the place. Was McPhee trying to pawn it off?"

Leary's lips were tight.

March stood. "My husband is dead," she said.

"Well, I don't speak ill of the dead," Roach said. "I'm sure you are feeling some loss. But after the funeral, how about you stop in here for some record-keeping? I'd like to know what that mine was producing, and whether that vein was pinching out, which is obviously what lies behind all this stuff. It looks like a scheme. But as I say, I'll speak no ill of the dead."

March ignored Leary's tight lips, and flared up. "So that's how it is, is it? Well, someone tried to kill me and my boy."

She scarcely knew where that had erupted from, but it sure quieted that little nook. There was a single-cell jail, mostly an alcove with iron bars, but it was empty. She wanted to throw Constable Roach into it and throw away the key.

"Come along, Mr. Leary; I'm done here. We're going to the newspaper. They'll write it up."

Roach stared, unmoving.

"I'll expect you at the funeral for my husband and son, Constable," she said. "I know you'll want to pay your respects."

With that, she headed for the street, with Leary at her heels.

"I always pay my respects," Roach said. "With interest added."

His great mustachios twitched like cat tails.

Outside, she smiled. Whenever life was out of kilter, she suddenly smiled. That was how she was. And Leary saw it, and smiled, too.

"So that's how you are," he said.

"His kinfolk are more important to him than justice, and he's not got a lick of kindness in his head," she said. "So now I have another enemy.

He's got nephews and a niece to protect, even if they decided they wanted a gold mine."

"Are you going to the *Beacon*?" he asked.

"With an obituary," she said. "Let him worry about a story for a few days. Let him fear the widow's word."

"You know, madam, and I hope you'll forgive me for saying it, but it's no longer about a gold mine someone's trying to nip from a widow. It's about a family's honor. That little copper, he's got it in his craw now. You're telling a story that makes his niece and nephews look bad. The three look like schemers and maybe killers, too. You've told a story that could put Roach's relatives in the state pen for a long time."

"If he's half a lawman, he'll look into it and do his duty."

"I would not want Roach making life painful for me," he said.

"Well, I thank you for your help, then."

"No, I didn't mean it that way, Mrs. McPhee. I'm in. I was speaking of his power to make life miserable for you. He has his ways. He's a rattler without rattles. He's in thick with the district judge, you know, and the pair have emptied the pockets of a lot of good people, including plenty of my customers. Now, you may think you're safe up there, at the mine, where the constable has no powers, but you'll be dead wrong. And that reminds me. You have no place. How are you going to live at the mine?"

"I don't know," she said. "But I will, and soon enough I'll see who comes for the gold, and I'll know who killed my son and tried to kill me."

FIVE

It was no easy thing to return to the mine.

"You shouldn't be there alone. Where'll you stay? What'll you eat? Who'll protect you?" the barkeep asked.

She dealt with him sternly. "Mr. Leary. I am thankful for your help. Now I will leave you and I'll manage."

"Sure, and there'll be another victim, this one a woman alone."

"You have your business to run, Mr. Leary. Yes, I like to be watched over, just as you did last night. I woke up, saw you sitting there, watching over me, and I knew what safety is. I will never forget it. But now I wish to be alone with my memories. It's what I need now."

She watched Tip Leary wrestle with it. Her intentions ran counter to his every instinct, and he couldn't let go of it.

"I'll come by and watch over you, then, and bring a little to eat. You have enemies, and they'll take advantage, and you need a man."

She was touched. "We're almost strangers, and I marvel that duty summons you so strongly. You are a fine man, Mr. Leary. The thing is, I'm a stubborn Scot, and there's nothing more bullheaded than a certain type of Scot, who's rooted into the ground like a hedgehog and won't budge."

He accepted the defeat. "You'll be calling on me, any hour, if there's a need, and I'll be doing what's in my powers. You have that from me."

She took his hand boldly. "I'll be looking for you at the mine, and you'll be welcome."

She left him there in the clay street. The morning was not even half spent. She felt his gaze upon her as she made her weary way to the far side of town, and turned off into Long Gulch, which would take her into the mountains.

She was inexpressibly weary, and scarcely noticed the vaulting slopes, the pine forest, the giant shoulders of the wilderness. But then she climbed the last grade and beheld the smoking ashes of her home, her life, and her baby.

She edged to the smoking ruin, dreading what she might see, but she saw nothing. The roof had collapsed, a pile of gray ash, covering everything. There was no sign of a crib. She walked over to the kitchen area, and found a few things she needed. Iron and steel did not perish. She found a Dutch oven, some knives and forks, a kettle, and other metal things, some pottery, too, some still too hot to touch, but things she would redeem.

She headed for Kermit's wagon, and knew she could live in it. The wagon had a roof and open sides, with roll-down canvas to keep out weather if needed. And then she worked her way to the root cellar that had been dug into a cool hollow that always felt like winter. There were potatoes, onions, tins of oats on a shelf. Food enough, if she could collect enough wood to cook it. And if she could start a fire. She had no matches but there would be whatever she needed at the mine—if Kermit's explosives hadn't been stolen.

She spent the next hours fashioning a camp. Except for clothing, she could manage for a while. Early in the afternoon Jerusalem Jones and Bum Carp appeared, along with a handcart and some shovels.

She studied them somberly as they wrestled the cart up the final grade. Were these the ones? She had every reason to fear them.

They eyed the smoldering pile of ash.

"Ma'am, we're come to fetch the late little baby for you," said the one she remembered as Jerusalem. "Mr. Laidlow sent us."

"Very well," she said.

They were eyeing her camp, the wagon, the metal things she had salvaged.

"Be about it quickly," she said. "I don't wish you to be here."

Jerusalem smiled. "Well, maybe we will. Mr. Laidlow, he sent along a little paper for you to sign. He says get it down, her signature, and then we're to do a bit of sifting here."

The cheerful young man handed her an envelope. She discovered a handwritten agreement within and a line where she was to sign it. The young man even had a bottle of black ink and a nib pen at the ready.

The agreement was a bill for two hundred and forty dollars, payable on signing to Laidlow Mortuary. But what followed got to the heart of it. If the bereaved could not come up with the funeral and burial expense, these could be satisfied with a half interest in her mine.

"So, that's the nettle," she said. "You may leave now."

"There'll be no funeral, then, ma'am."

"Do what you will with my husband."

"You'll still owe, ma'am, for what's been done. He's been prepared, for fifty dollars."

"Go!"

The pair of them were smiling, blandly.

"We'd like to fetch your little one from the ashes," Bum said. "Put the dear little tyke to rest, good and proper, just as a mother would wish."

"Go!" she yelled.

But they were in no hurry. They strolled about, noting her wagon and what she had salvaged.

"You will leave now. This is private property," she said.

But they lingered, taking inventory, while her temper built up in her.

"Bring my husband here and I will bury him here," she said.

That startled the pair, but didn't achieve much.

They simply grinned, and continued their inventory of the place. But then, at long last, they called it quits.

"We'll be taking whatever we can find, to satisfy the debt, ma'am."

Bum swept up the Dutch oven and kettle and tableware, and dumped it all in the cart.

"Stop that!" she cried, and bulled toward them, but Jerusalem caught her arm and held tight even as she wrestled to free herself.

Bum pulled a jackknife from his pocket, freed the canvas from the wagon, rolled it up, and put it in the handcart, in effect destroying the only shelter she might have there.

"You'll be wanting to pay Mr. Laidlow his rightful reward for services," Jerusalem said, and let her go.

They smiled, bowed, and headed leisurely down the grade, pushing the handcart laden with the few precious things that she needed to survive far from town.

She watched furiously. She was angry, but she was sickened, too. The episode had revealed how vulnerable she was; how fragile her life in that wagon might be; how easily she might be coerced or brutalized or starved or bullied.

They were gone. She stared down the peaceful trail to the gulch below. The birds were singing. The countryside had restored itself.

There would be no service, no burial. What the

mortician would do she could not imagine, but she guessed the county would bury her husband in a potter's field.

She had nothing. She could not stay.

In the space of a day, she had lost everything. And all because of a small gold mine. They wanted her gone. They meant to possess it. Drive her away. She struggled with that. All she had to do was walk down that long grade and into Marysville, and soon enough life would sort itself out. She would survive there, make friends, get help, begin anew, maybe enter a trade or domestic service. She would endure and build and create a new life.

Only she was stubborn, Scots-born, and bullheaded.

She needed a shelter, food and clothing, and a shotgun. There might still be some of those things lying about.

She eyed the still-smoldering ruin of her cabin, now the grave of her child as well as her every dream, and she let go of it. That life was gone. She did not start for town. She hiked up the steep grade to the mine head, high on a bleak slope that vaulted into rocky ridges. She felt the fine clear air and blessing of sun on the countryside. It was foolish to think she owned any of it. Foolish to think that predators would respect the four corner cairns, the discovery cairn, and the patent that her husband had gotten from the government of the United States. They would take it all away.

But she was what she was. It wasn't for the mine that she was willful, but because of the principle of the thing. She could sign away her rights, collect a pittance, and start a new life. But she was damned if she would.

She studied the disorderly mine head, and swiftly realized that the mine was not entirely sealed. The explosion had tumbled a lot of rock into the small shaft, but there was a place of darkness, a place where the rubble had not reached the top, a place where a woman might crawl into the shaft, if she were gentle and careful, and gouge out gold-bearing quartz. A place of shelter, rough and cruel as it might be.

What else was there? A powder magazine fifty yards off. An ore car now inside the blocked mine. A shed nearby, and in it some of Kermit's work clothing—faded flannel shirts, old britches, some work boots—which gladdened her. And to her unbelieving eyes, a surprise. A shotgun stood behind a hanging pair of pants. He had told her of it, told her it was something needful at a mine, but she had forgotten it. She studied the big thing, uncertain whether she could lift and shoot it. It was a simple, one-barrel weapon, with a box of shells tucked into a corner.

She found a steel bucket and wiped it clean. A tin kettle. Spoons and a knife for delicate work. A tin cup. A tin plate. She eyed a variety of tools, including an ax and maul and sledgehammer, drilling steels, a pike and crowbar, several shovels, some rope, and a box of kitchen matches. A tarpaulin lay on the floor. She found a crimping tool used to anchor fuse to a cap.

In the powder magazine she found half a crate of DuPont Hercules dynamite. Nearby, she found Bickford fuse and a box of copper-jacketed caps. She would hide these things. They would make a better weapon than the heavy shotgun. She had never worked with these explosives, but she had listened to Kermit talk about them often enough. And had watched him, a time or two, which he hated.

This would be her salvation. But first she had to crawl into the shaft, if she could. She eyed the rubble, looking for dangerous rock, and concluded that gravity had settled it in the mouth of the shaft. At the tool shed, she slipped out of her borrowed blue dress and climbed into Kermit's too-large flannel shirt and britches, and belted the pants tight, hoping they would stay up on her generous hips. They did. She eased onto the rubble, felt rocks slip and quake under her, and finally reached the open space, shaped like a quarter moon at the top.

Acrid air greeted her. She would need fresh, which meant she must enlarge that opening, rock by rock, until she and air could enter freely. So she set to work, mostly by prying rock loose with the pike and letting it slide down. It soon wore her out, especially when she wrestled with a large piece, too heavy to budge. She wished for a lot more strength, but wishing wouldn't help her any, so she pried and hammered and gradually enlarged the opening until she had cleared a three-foot-high passage.

She crawled in, her body hurting as she fought past the rock barrier, and finally she eased into the mine. The air was bad, but worse, she was totally uncomfortable in there, with only a little daylight to guide her. Gold, it seemed, was next door to hell, and probably for a good reason. She feared that more rock would fall on her, pin her, kill her.

She ached to escape, and found getting out was as treacherous as clambering in, and when she finally did escape, she was scraped and bruised. But she welcomed the sun, and the great blue dome above. She was not meant to live in the shaft of a gold mine. Her hope of quietly gouging enough gold-laden quartz from the mine to keep her fed and clothed had vanished.

She had a decision to make. Stay or leave. She could simply drift into town and see what employment she could find. She could abandon the place to those predators. Maybe all that gold wasn't worth it. Or she could stay there, defend the mine, live a lonely life, grow desperate for food and succor, wage a hopeless fight to hang on to Kermit's gold mine. All for what?

She might last a week or two.

She could come to no decision. But there were a few things she might do. Slowly, painfully, she carried all the mining equipment from the head of the mine and hid it in her root cellar. When she had finished, that cellar contained the Hercules dynamite, the tools from the shed, the tarpaulin, the shirts and britches, the iron pail, the shotgun and shells, and all the rest. She shut the door and found some brush to conceal it, and stared at her handiwork. She was weary and discouraged. Still, that cache of food and equipment might be valuable some day soon.

SIX

Something about her changed. Ever since the hour when she had slipped into Kermit's plaid flannel shirt and canvas pants, which she had to roll up a bit, she discovered she wasn't the same. She was the woman she had always been, but the freedom of men's clothing, the pants instead of a skirt, made life easier. She couldn't explain it; there were no words to describe this sudden influx of selfhood. It was almost as if Kermit had become a resident alongside herself.

Restlessly, she began to patrol the lode claim, fifteen hundred by six hundred feet, running up the side of the mountain, embracing gulches and ridges, forest and outcropped rock. The discovery shaft lay near the bottom. Above, forested slopes catapulted upward. She wasn't quite sure where the corner cairns were, demarcating the rectangular boundaries of the McPhee Mine. She would find them.

She would find a place to call a refuge. She didn't need a shelter. That was one of the odd changes she felt. Before, in skirts, she ached for a cabin, a roof over her, stout log walls, warmth and a good bed. Now, in Kermit's pants, she didn't need a shelter for a while. She had the old mining tarpaulin for cover and warmth, and that would do until autumn. If someone had asked her how she felt this hour, she simply would have replied that she enjoyed the freedom of pants.

She found no good refuge on the mining property, but a little south, along the rocky flank of the mountain, she found a protected ledge, with an overhang that turned it into an open-sided cave. Mountain lion scat told her it was much used by animals. It had wood nearby for fire, a ridge and forest for a screen so she could keep a fire without being seen, and easy access to the McPhee Mine.

At least until her food ran out, she could live in nature, invisible, a wraith unseen by the gold-fevered people who even now were casting their covetous eyes upon the mine. With the shotgun she might even be able to feed herself. And maybe Tip Leary would help her. As she worked to create a refuge, she gave thought to what would come next.

Who wanted the mine so badly?

There was the Constable, Roach, and the funeral man Laidlow, and Jerusalem Jones and Bum Carp. There might be the assayer, Wittgenstein, though she trusted him more than the others. There might be all sorts of ruthless people itching to steal a mine, people who would scruple at nothing.

She retrieved the tools and some of the food from her root cellar. It was the second time she had moved them that day. She was glad to abandon the cabin, which had become the grave of her baby and the death of her dreams. Let them think she had vanished, or left the country, or even died somewhere. There would be a parade of people who would wander around the burned cabin, and walk up to the mine, and peer into its mostly blocked shaft, and dream of tearing more gold out of the rock.

That eve, after boiling some potatoes in the iron pail, she taught herself to load and unload the shotgun, and then settled on a pine bough bed beneath Kermit's old tarpaulin. She fell asleep almost instantly, still in her flannel shirt and britches. In a way, March McPhee had disappeared from the world.

At the mine the next morning, she made some *No Trespassing* signs, using axle grease and black ash for paint. These she posted at the mine head, the burnt-out cabin, and at the foot of the property, where the trail entered the patented lode claim. The sign at the base also had the words, *Private Property* daubed on them. They might not stop anyone, but they laid legal ground for whatever would follow. She spent the remainder of that day sifting through the ruin of her cabin for whatever might be useful, but there was little of value.

She was alone, but not lonely. At least not yet. March had no intention of living out her life as some shadowy wilderness catamount, scarcely seen by the world. She would continue here until it was time to leave, which probably would be when those who tried to kill her were brought to justice.

She spotted a man laboring up the trail, and knew at once it was Tipperary Leary, her rescuer. It puzzled her. He opened his saloon at noon, and it was past that.

He was unfamiliar with these precincts, and eyed the burned-out cabin, finally discovering her standing quietly.

"So, I found you then," he said, his gaze focused on her pants and shirt.

"You're a long way from Marysville," she said.

"I said I'd keep watch over you, and so I will."

"But your saloon—you open at noon."

"I'll open when I'm good and ready. It'll improve the livers of my customers. You lack clothing, then."

"I am in Kermit's. It frees me up. A dress is a bother."

"It's not good, you wearing pants and all. I am hoping this will pass."

"It's no business of yours, Mr. Leary. And I hardly have a rag to my name."

Chastened, he cleared his throat and stared at the gloomy pile of ash that once had been a home. "I thought I'd see about you, that's all. There's things I hear—a barkeep hears more than most— and let you know. Now here's a thing: Your man's going to be buried tomorrow, I hear. Laidlow's going to give him a fancy sendoff, and charge you for it, and it'll be a claim against your mine. He's got an angle. So, eleven o'clock is the hour."

"I did not authorize it, so it's no claim upon me, Mr. Leary."

Leary stared into the unfamiliar blue of the heavens, and then proceeded. "Mrs. McPhee, I know a few things about the town. There's a lot of people from across the sea here. There's a clan—relatives, cousins, in-laws—all got together to squeeze what they can from whoever they've got in their crosshairs. Some are in Helena, some here. Mostly they go after the Micks like me. They're all related. There's Roach, the constable; Laidlow and his bunch; the Joneses; the Carps; and some Mortimers, the merchant family. They're mean, they're hard, but a little shy of outright crooks. Word is—and I heard plenty the last evening or two—they want this mine and they'll take it, and if you resist, you're mincemeat."

"Then I'll avoid them."

"Ah, it won't play out that way, Mrs. McPhee. They'll make sure of it."

He gazed somberly at her, and she knew he was right. The last thing she wanted was some sort of war. But they had already started one, with the purpose of stealing her gold mine, and there was no way she could escape what was coming.

"Thank you, Mr. Leary. You've told me truly. I'm a stubborn woman. It's in the blood. I'll see to it that they are repaid. I repay with interest. If they do me a favor, I will repay it; if they do me harm, that, too, will be repaid in full."

"Mrs. McPhee, madam, it would be your ruin, forgive me for saying it."

"Then I will be ruined, Mr. Leary. They started this, you know. They sealed the mine. That keeps others out of it, and the ore in it. That also keeps me from selling the mine. No one would buy it if he can't see the ore, the vein, the prospects. So that was their first step. And the second, done a few moments after the blast, was to burn me out. They caught my son, but I was not inside. They intended to leave the mine without an owner. You say they're a little shy of outright crooks, sir, but that's not it. They're hooligans of the worst sort. They might look respectable, but they aren't."

"There, you see? You'll want to think this out, madam."

"You've done that for me, and I'm glad of it. Tell me, is Mr. Wittgenstein, the assayer, one of them?"

"No, not at all."

"I didn't think so. He's been a friend of my husband and will be mine as well."

"Mrs. McPhee, you're one lone woman."

"Would I be better off if I were one lone man?"

"Well, I'm thinking, maybe yes, forgive me please."

"Come with me, Mr. Leary, and we'll have some tea in my hideaway. It's a little bit up from here."

"No, with thanks, but it's overdue for me to head down to the tavern and let all those poor thirsting wretches through the doors, so they can get their foot up on the bar rail, as usual."

She smiled.

"I hear plenty, madam. I sometimes know what's what, and sometimes what's going to happen. I will keep you posted. And if you want for anything, like real female clothing that restore you to what is right and natural in the universe, I will do it."

"Medium," she said.

"Medium what?"

"Medium height, waist, shoulders."

He smiled. It was odd how rarely he smiled. But she liked the sudden brightness in his eyes. "A whole wardrobe for my friend, Mrs. McPhee," he said.

She watched him tenderly as he made his way down the grade. He had come a long way to tell her a few things and to look after her. He was used to walking—barkeeps walked a great deal—but not used to steep grades. He seemed different there at the mine, lonely and out of his element. Less confident than in the town, where he was entirely at home. It was good to have friends like Tip Leary, people who watched over her.

Should she go to the unauthorized funeral? She decided she should. She ached to do right for Kermit, to bury him with respect and honor.

Maybe his spirit would know it, would see it, would thank her. She didn't know for certain about an afterlife. For years she had tried to reinforce a belief in heaven by reciting these things by rote, and then she realized it did her no good. She wasn't sure. She wasn't at all confident that she would reach another life, and find her husband in another life, and live in eternal bliss somewhere or other.

She slept uneasily that night. A sharp breeze told her that a hideaway under an overhang of rock would not spare her from cold and wind, or even rain. By dawn she was drawn and worn.

She washed at a nearby runnel, and slipped into the blue dress, which was stained and ill suited. But it would have to do. She would attend her husband's funeral. When the sun was warming the bottom of the gulch, she headed toward Marysville and whatever her fate might be.

She headed straight for Laidlow's, unnoticed in a humdrum morning, and straightaway entered the chapel, which was banked with lilacs. She was alone. A burnished oak casket with expensive furniture stood closed. Her heart melted. Therehe was, the man who had cleaved to her and wrought a life together for her and him. The man whose dream she had shared. The man who smiled at her while he ate his porridge. There he was, gone, the lid of the casket hiding the crushed ruin of his face and mangle of his body and arms and legs.

"You came, Mrs. McPhee."

She whirled to find Mortimer Laidlow, gotten up in a swallowtail and starched white shirt, behind her.

She wanted to blister him, say that she had not authorized any of it, would not pay for it, didn't owe anything for it, and would sign nothing. But the presence of death changes everything.

"This is right," she said.

"It's a little early. Perhaps you'd like to look over the contract before the ceremony, and get all that out of the way."

She nodded, and he led her into that asphyxiating little alcove back in the mortuary.

The contract was just as before; if she could not pay, she would deed him half of the McPhee Mine as payment in full.

She would not sign. "I will assume the debt, and find a way to repay it. I will not deed any part of my mine to you, in any circumstances, sir. Two hundred and eighty dollars will be paid to you when I am ready; the mine will not change ownership."

He seemed oddly content with that, and she wondered what was running through his mind. Surely he had a dozen angles, and she scarcely knew any of them. She knew little about liens, and supposed that was what he had in mind.

But at least Kermit would be buried.

SEVEN

It was a proper funeral. March was escorted to a front pew; before her was the fine casket of burnished hardwood, with brass furniture. Bouquets flanked the chapel altar. A frail, bent minister unknown to her, the Reverend Mr. Pinkerton, recited the usual prayers, condolences, and hope of eternal life in some unfathomable place. He did not know Kermit.

Behind her sat just two people: Constable Roach, and the assayer, Mr. Wittgenstein, bald, bespectacled, and wreathed in black. Mr. Laidlow hovered at the doors along with his flunkies; Mistletoe, Jerusalem Jones, and Bum Carp. The latter had been recruited as pallbearers. March wondered whether they had also been recruited to burn her to death in her cabin.

The assayer, alone among those attending the funeral, came to honor Kermit.

March felt discomfited by her blue dress, gotten from a lady of the streets, misshapen and unclean. But maybe it didn't matter. She was present, no matter how she was clad.

"May I offer the pulpit to anyone who wishes to eulogize Mr. McPhee?" the divine asked.

March found herself rising and walking up two steps, and then facing the empty chapel. She didn't know what she would say. She wanted Kermit buried within a cocoon of blessings and kindness.

She was aware of how ill-kempt she was, but somehow it didn't matter. What counted was Kermit.

"My husband, Kermit McPhee, grew up in Edinburgh, Scotland, and attended the university there. He graduated with a degree in geology. His gaze was always on the horizon, and soon he emigrated here, bringing me, his bride, with him.

"He was not afraid of hard labor or physical hardship, and saw opportunity in the North American continent, as yet little explored and much of it unmapped. I came with him gladly, proud to be married to a man who wished to advance through life on his merits and industry, through his skills and knowledge, through his integrity and courage.

"So he prospected for minerals, located the present mine, and followed your laws scrupulously, proving his claim and winning a patent, which he shared with me. There were things he scorned. He had no use for people who tried to snatch wealth from others through questionable means. Such people, he felt, were not real men; they were parasites, feasting on the courage and industry and wisdom of others. He believed in honest industry, and did what he believed in.

"He had a great heart, a rare courage, and a

kindness that brought him friendship and trust from others. I can put it simply: he was an honorable man, and that separated him from those whose entire enterprise is to snatch away what others have won.

"I shall miss him. I will visit his grave now and then, refreshing my understanding of what is good about the human race because he was a good and true man. He loved me. He supported me. He nurtured a family. He also inspired me, and his legacy to me is the wish to live as he did, with courage, kindness, and honor."

She gazed at the small audience, at the ones who would not meet her gaze eye to eye, but seemed to stare at the ceiling.

"We are burying this day a fine man," she said. "And the man I love."

And returned to her pew.

She had not started her eulogy to deliver a message but that was how it ended up. She knew she had forced those who heard her to consider their own conduct. Maybe it would do them some good.

The service ended with a simple blessing, and she found herself in a cortège carrying her husband to his grave. He would not have approved of the coffin or the funeral. But what was done was done, and that was how his life on earth would end.

The Marysville cemetery had few graves in it because of the rawness of the town, but one was ready for Kermit. Laidlow's two young men eased the coffin into the gray earth, and off a way Constable Roach watched. The constable was determined to see everything and miss nothing.

March left a red rose on the coffin, a rose supplied by the funeral home, and then they took her back to the funeral parlor, and she was free to go where she would.

Except that Constable Roach intercepted her.

"Mrs. McPhee, follow me, please."

She did, and he took her to his alcove in the city hall, and bade her sit down.

He carefully removed his blue hat and eyed her, his mustache twitching.

"You are by definition a vagrant," he said. "We have a law that forbids vagrants from loitering in Marysville. The law defines a vagrant as a person without visible means and without a residence and without funds and without moral or ethical scruple. You have no means, no residence, and no funds. You qualify. I will not hold you this time, because of your loss, but if you should enter my town again, I will be forced to place you in that cage there for a day and fine you two dollars and confiscate anything you possess and evict you from this peaceful community. That's all I have to say."

He rose.

"Don't ever propose marriage," she said, and laughed.

It was so unexpected and gamey that all she could do was whoop. He turned red, his rheumy eyes blazed, and she could see he itched to pitch her into the cell then and there. But some sobriety returned, and he simply nodded curtly.

"You might lock yourself up and fine yourself and banish yourself from Marysville," she said, stepping into fresh spring air.

She headed for the assay office, hoping Mr. Wittgenstein had returned. She entered, which triggered a cowbell, and soon enough he emerged from a small rear room, dressed in his laboratory smock once again.

"Well, well, Mrs. McPhee," he said, uncertainly.

"I wish to thank you for paying your respects," she said.

"He was a remarkable man, Mrs. McPhee. And had he lived, I believe he would have prospered. The mine was getting better and better."

"It is for sale, sir. Do you know of a reputable buyer?"

"I'd buy it myself if I had the means. But you may be in for a difficult time, because the mouth has been blown shut and there are parties who'll do whatever they can to prevent a sale, and delay or discourage you in every way."

She stared.

"I think you know that," he said gently.

"I think my little eulogy reached the right ears," she said.

At that point some understanding passed between them.

"Following the burial, the constable invited me to his warren and told me I'm a vagrant and will be fined and jailed if I return to Marysville."

Wittgenstein stared, amazed.

"Well, I am a vagrant," she said. "No home, no funds, no visible income or position or connection."

"Mrs. McPhee," he said. "You happen to possess a gold mine with great promise. People come to me all the time, offering me a reward if I reveal the tenor of the McPhee ore I've assayed. Only yesterday, several people approached me, nearly all of them relatives of our worthy constable. At one point, this place was broken into. Since then I've kept all my assays of the McPhee Mine under lock and key. I also reported the break-in to Constable Roach, telling him I've notified the county sheriff as well. That served as a warning."

His manner became very gentle, his voice low and soft.

"There are people here who mean to take the mine from you by rook or crook. Frankly, they're a clan plus a few in-laws. They're all in tight. Mortimer Laidlow is the godfather. He's a careful one and always has the younger ones doing his dirty work. I've seen it. An assayer can't help but see it. They'll try to steal it, or do it with intimidation, or lawsuit, or bribery, or whatever. Actually, they were circling your husband, but he was not a man to be bullied. I confess, when I heard of his death, I wondered if it had been arranged, but that is most unlikely. He didn't timber his shaft, even in fragmented rock, and paid a terrible price for his daring."

"I begged him to."

"Once, he told me it'd put his mine in the red. He'd do it, after it was showing a tidy profit."

She felt an odd tenderness. "Mr. Wittgenstein, what should I do?"

He shook his head. "I wish I knew. People without scruple will never cease to alarm or hurt you to get the prize. I think I would call Roach's bluff. You might well go back there, now, and tell him you're going to stay in town, and if he wants to arrest you, go ahead."

"And what if he does?"

"This town, Mrs. McPhee, would laugh the man out of office."

"Unless I rot in there undiscovered."

"I am standing ready. It happens I do the assays for the Drumlummon. A word from me will be heard."

Thomas Cruse's great mine was the sole reason Marysville existed. A little pressure from the powerful men who ran it would go far.

"Do you think my mine will support me?"

He shook his head. "I'm not a geologist. There are dozens of factors. The vein might pinch out tomorrow. The ore might not reduce well. The mine might flood. The price of gold might decline. But I can say this: his assays got better and better, and he told me his vein got thicker and wider as he bored in." He smiled. "That's the heart of it."

"I wish I knew what to do," she said.

"I wish I could help you with that," he said. "I'm a chemist, not a swami."

"I've just assumed a heavy debt, burying Kermit. He would be horrified."

"Yes, and they'll use it as a lever."

"Do you know someone willing to buy it straight off—for what it's worth?"

"No one knows what it's worth, I'm afraid."

"There's nothing now. Nothing keeping me up at my mine but the wish to sell it properly." Then she added a caveat. "And no one's going to push me off."

"Then the way to do that is to share in its profits. Find a partner. Make sure he's square. Gold does things even to men who start out with a head full of ethics."

"Would you?"

He sighed, smiled and shook his head. "I know my profession very well; buying and managing mines is quite beyond my abilities. I come from an Austrian family known for its suicides, so I live without high ambition."

She felt weary. The funeral had drained her of her last reserves. "Mr. Wittgenstein, thank you for coming. Thank you for, well, looking after me. You've helped in ways I can't explain."

He nodded, and lifted a white work smock from its peg on the wall. "I like to think I'm good for a few things," he said. "Not just chemistry."

She stepped into the fresh spring air, walked back to the building that housed city offices and Constable Roach's prim warren.

He looked up at her, started. His revolver lay in pieces on a table. He had been cleaning it.

"Well, here I am," she said. "The vagrant is staying in Marysville."

"It seems you're begging for trouble."

"Go ahead. Arrest the vagrant who is a widow with a gold mine. Arrest the vagrant with the fifteen hundred by six hundred foot patented, proven lode mine."

He did nothing.

"Mr. Roach, I don't even know your given name. Is it Herald? Donald?"

"For you, it's Constable."

"Have you held this office long?"

He reddened slowly, and fidgeted with his fingers, and looked exactly like a man being bested.

"Here," she said. "Go ahead."

She walked into the cell and waited. She saw the heat boil through him. He was a man not at all used to being thwarted or crossed. But some innate caution slowly cooled him down, and he did not leap from his stool and slam the barred-iron door shut.

"Thank you, peace officer," she said, and stepped out. "If you owned a gold mine, I'd do the same for you. You wouldn't qualify for vagrant. Not even after arsonists burnt your home. Which is something well understood in this town. Now I will task you. Find out who set my home ablaze. And arrest them for premeditated taking of life."

"Not my jurisdiction," he muttered.

"And not your inclination," she said. "You might be related."

The look on his face, as she walked into fresh air, was one she would never forget, and one that she knew would torment her dreams. She thought maybe she had pushed him too far, and would pay a price for it. She had pointed at his clan.

EIGHT

The *No Trespassing* notice at the edge of her property was missing. She stormed up the trail to the mine, and found three men hard at work mucking rock out of the mine shaft. They were young, burly, and knew what they were doing.

They had cleared the shaft, piled the rock to one side, and were putting Kermit's ore car back into operation.

They spotted her, but barely stopped working.

"You are on my property, and you must leave," she said.

They ignored her.

"This is private property. You are trespassing."

"Sorry lady, we're taking over," said one. He was the smallest of the three, ferret-faced, full of itchy energy that made him unable to stand still. The other two ignored her, cleaning out the rock from the ore car.

"Your name, sir?" she asked.

"Call me Poker. Call him Three-Card Monte. Call that one Faro. We just hit the jackpot, wouldn't you say?"

They all paused, grinning at her, knowing they held the high cards.

"Looks like an abandoned mine to me," Poker said. "All shut down, no one around. Dead mines, they're fair game. No one owns 'em. So we done took it."

"Lady, you're trespassing. This here is now our claim," said Three-Card Monte.

"Yeah, and if you don't, no telling what'll happen to you. Can't say as you'd like it," added Faro.

That one was big and smirky and grinning.

She understood the threat. And it riled her.

She headed down the grade, but then turned off toward her refuge, where Kermit's shotgun was waiting for her. She needed a double-barreled one, but this would have to do. What she planned to do might be reckless, but it had to be done.

She hastened along an invisible trail on the slope, through dense timber, and then to her ledge under the overhanging rock where her few small possessions were hidden. She found the twelve-gauge shotgun, checked the load, pocketed half a dozen shells, and headed back.

By the time she reached the mine head, they had gotten the mine opened, and two of the three had vanished, no doubt into the shaft. The third, Three-Card Monte, was urinating on the rock pile.

"Hands up," she said, enjoying his dilemma.

They were slow to rise.

"Do it. This is buckshot and it will cut you in two."

"Aw, lady, you hardly know how to hold that

thing. I bet you never pointed a gun in your sweet little life," he said.

His hands did not reach for the heavens.

"Button up and then walk in front of me. We're going to Marysville," she said.

He grinned, sat down, and didn't budge.

He had read her well. She was not ready to kill the man in cold blood, and he knew it. There were proper ways to deal with this, and shooting an unarmed trespasser was not one of them. She felt a sudden flood of frustration.

He stood, slowly. He eyed her, eyed the shotgun, and stepped toward her.

"You're going to give me that gun, lady," he said, moving one step at a time, closer and closer.

She aimed at his knees and pulled the trigger. The shotgun bucked violently, knocking her back. Three-Card Monte howled, collapsed, as blood blossomed on his lower legs.

She was shocked at herself.

He sat howling. Both of his legs gouted bright blood.

She ejected the shell and slipped in another and snapped the shotgun together.

The other two erupted from the mine, took it all in with a glance, and studied her shotgun.

"Patch him up and carry him off, and don't come back," she said.

They saw the blood, the howling man, and

nodded. She let them reach the wounded man and start to bind him up with their shirts. She watched, her shotgun leveled. One of the balls had hit a kneecap. Two others had cut into his calves. Three-Card's mining days were probably over.

"Next time, I'll aim higher," she said.

The injured man coughed and sobbed. The other two got the bleeding more or less slowed, but the wounded man was wailing, an eerie howl that sent shivers through her.

She watched them load the man into a wheelbarrow, ignoring the picks and sledges and shovels they had brought, and slowly wheel the man down the mountain. The three card sharks never looked back.

She sat at the mine head, shaking. She had shot a man. Gold had fevered her, along with the rest. It was hard to swallow, inflicting so much pain upon the man, even if he was robbing her and defying her. If she had been a man would he have ignored her as he had? She didn't know. It didn't matter. She was simply March McPhee, and she would do whatever she must to preserve her property and her life.

But it had been almost as shattering for her as it had been for the one calling himself Three-Card Monte. And yet there was a difference. She would not kill if she could help it. She was not born to womanhood to take life, but to nurture it. If she could defend her property without taking life, she would. That was the difference. She would not stoop to the level her adversaries had reached, reckless of life. She had her pride.

She wondered whose men they were, whether they, too, were part of Laidlow's clan, doing the first dirtywork. Or whether they were simply opportunists, a threesome who heard all the gossip in one of the saloons, and decided that some bold marauding might get them a gold mine. Maybe it didn't matter. What did matter was what to do next, and how to defend herself.

Maybe Tip Leary could help her. She wanted to talk to him. It was a marvel how much a barkeep knew. He would soon know all about Poker and his friends, and what their fate had been, and what sort of new troubles she faced. There was something tender in Tip Leary, and she saw something in his gaze that he wanted to hide from her, and she knew what it was, and it actually caused her to smile.

The mine shaft was wide open again. She could walk in if she wanted. And so could anyone else. The glint of the thin rails vanished in the gloom. She was afraid to go in there. The working face wasn't far, but it was all too far for her. This tunnel into the mountain drew men of all sorts, men who would do anything to seize the gold threading the vein of milky quartz that kept getting wider and wider. It was a hungry man's dream. Gold, gold, not far in, easy to tear out of the mountain.

A bonanza, fit for a king, and nothing but a widow in the way.

She pushed the ore car into the shaft and let it rest there as a barrier. They would be coming now, wave after wave, and she had only moral suasion and perhaps the courts to stop them—if the judges were upright. She thought they might be. But what good was it? She hadn't a nickel to hire a lawyer.

She spotted the picks and sledgehammers and shovels the three had left behind, and these she collected and hid in a nearby gully, out of sight. There was no point in leaving the tools of robbery around for the next invader to use.

Then, weary, she made her way to her refuge, and there she changed from her borrowed blue dress into her husband's flannel shirt and britches. And once again she marveled at the change in her: it was no longer necessary to walk and sit decorously. A man could walk any way he pleased.

There was something she had to do, and she didn't know where she would find the courage. She had to pierce the work face of Kermit's mine, and chip enough quartz out to take to Marysville now and then for food and necessaries. She hated the thought of it, but without a little cash her determination to stay on the mine property and defend it was nothing but fantasy. The very idea terrified her, but she knew she would do it, make herself walk in there step by step, and chip out the quartz. She returned to the solemn shaft, basking in bright sun, and peered in. She had the tools in hand: a burlap sack, a pry bar, pickhammer, and Kermit's carbide lamp.

She studied the silent mountains, looking for signs of human beings, but the mine slumbered in the June warmth. She eyed the roof of the shaft, with its jagged, broken rock that should be supported with timbering. Maybe she could poke it, hit it, make it fall ahead of her if it was going to drop. She started the acetylene lamp going, and stepped in. The initial dozen feet were solid enough, but the next twenty were plainly fragmented strata, and this worried her.

She tapped it, and a few small pieces dropped, startling her. She tapped again, sometimes hard, but nothing happened. That gave her a little courage, and she dared to go another few feet and do it all again. But she failed to unloose anything ahead of her, and gradually she worked along the shaft, even as daylight faded behind her, until there it was, the face, the thick milky seam laced with wire and nodule gold. Her heart hammered, and she decided to be quick about it. She worked feverishly, prying pieces of the rotted quartz loose and dropping them into her burlap sack. It was hard going, and sometimes she jammed a pry bar in and moved nothing.

And then, somehow, she had as much quartz as she could drag out, and she tugged it along on the rough surface, step by step, foot by foot, until sunlight blinded her and alpine breezes began to cleanse her face and cool her body. She never was so glad to see sunlight. She studied the flat, the copses of pine, the tumbling slope, the silent ore car, and saw no one. She slid over to the gully and hid her tools.

She didn't know what to do with her heavy bag of quartz. Kermit had rented a mule now and then and hauled his quartz to the Drumlummon mill, which crushed it and removed the tiny bits of gold through an amalgamation process she was hazy about. But she knew it used mercury to pluck the gold from the crushed rock. She would need to get that heavy load to town, where Mr. Wittgenstein would help her. There in that quartz was gold to sustain her, but as long as it was locked in, it would get her nothing.

She knew a little about these things. Kermit had always talked about them, wanting her to know about their mine. But she only half-listened; operating a mine was scarcely on her mind. But now she wished she had listened more. She dragged the sack of quartz down to the burnt-out cabin and hid it nearby. The great heap of ash wrought a sadness in her, along with a flood of memories of Kermit, of meals gotten from a cranky woodstove, of tender moments and winter moments when they were snowed in and Kermit couldn't even climb the path to his mine.

Now she was wearing his pants.

She wished she had a dog. She needed one to alert her to anyone coming up her trail. Wilderness is quiet, and people and animals pass through it in utter silence. She was about to head for her refuge, the protected ledge, when she did spot a man laboring up the trail. The blue suit was familiar to her, along with the wiry frame. It was not someone she welcomed.

She collected the shotgun and waited. She was tempted to vanish; there was still time to plunge into the forest and escape. But she elected to stay and see this through, whatever it was.

When he reached the burnt-out cabin, she stepped into view, which startled him.

He examined her closely, noting the flannel shirt and britches, and also the old shotgun.

"You fired that thing," he said. "Pretty near killed a man, in-law relative of mine."

"He was trespassing and wouldn't go. And he was also stealing my ore, and wouldn't stop."

"You shot him."

"Through the legs."

"You've crippled him."

"I was defending myself."

"You maybe took his livelihood away from him. That's a hard thing."

"He was taking my livelihood and property from me. He was stealing. And he refused to leave. He and the others, who were in my mine."

"Don't make no difference. I'm taking you in."

"This is not your jurisdiction. You said so yourself."

"I go where I need to go to get justice done."

"Get a sheriff and a warrant, if that's what's needed."

"You're getting a little too smart, I think. Woman running around in pants."

"Maybe you should run around in skirts, and see what it makes you."

Some feral hatred bloomed in his eyes.

"Get off my property," she said, lifting the shotgun a notch.

He grinned suddenly, but it was wolfish.

"You coming in with me, proper and lawful?"

"What you're doing isn't proper. And not lawful."

"Guess we'll see about that," he said.

"Don't come back," she said.

He was slow to leave, lingering, mocking, and only the shotgun stood between her and him. But then he left.

NINE

March watched the ebony buggy pulled by an ebony horse climb the steep road toward the mine. The buggy carried one person, its driver, who was swathed in a black suit, and seemed at that distance to have shiny black hair.

She saw no sign of a weapon. Indeed, the man looked to be a gentleman of means, perhaps a professional. Certainly he was well attired, in a gray cravat and polished black boots, a gold watch fob dangling from his waistcoat.

The dray struggled up the last fifty yards, where the road curved around a shoulder and then stopped at the little flat where her burned cabin lay in a heap.

She felt oddly intimidated. No such elegantly dressed person had ever visited the McPhee Mine. She had taken to wearing Kermit's pants and shirts because they were suited for the hard work she was doing. She had created a sort of outside living area, employing the salvaged woodstove for her meals, which were drawing down what lay in her root cellar.

But curiosity prevailed, and she strode toward the slightly dusty buggy as its owner pulled the dray to a halt. She did not neglect to carry her shotgun. It had become as intimate to her as a spare limb, and she was never far from it.

He lifted a black derby, and eyed her with warm, spaniel eyes, all the while examining her whole self, the camp, and the ruined cabin.

"You're Mrs. McPhee," he said. "Permit me to introduce myself. I am Hermes Apollo, a practitioner of law. My mother couldn't decide whether it was Hermes or Apollo who fathered me, so she named me after both suspects. She lived in a world of her own. May I have a brief visit with you?"

"Why don't you just sit there on that quilted leather seat, and tell me?" she asked.

"I would feel discomfited, my nether regions resting in comfort while yours are perched on a stump. But I am at your service."

"That's what I'm afraid of. I'll give you one minute to lay it out."

"Madam, dire events are descending on you. Word is, in Marysville, that you will be hauled into assorted Territorial courts, where creditors intend to attach your mine, or prove that its patent is invalid, or prove that claims were filed on that lode prior to your husband's. In short, the jackals are looking for carrion, and I propose to be your knight."

"I'll probably have it sold to a reputable buyer before they all start the tango," she said.

"Ah, madam, you are innocent of human nature."

"So I am. That's why I keep a shotgun handy."

"I noticed it. A handy instrument, but of little value in a world of torts. No, madam, you need much more."

"And what is your price, sir?"

"Absolutely nothing. I have admired you from afar, often envying your late husband for his great good fortune, and now my every wish, to be of service to you, is coming true."

March chewed on that one for a while, and didn't quite know which point on the compass it was leading. But she was damned if she'd be any man's mistress.

"Sorry," she said. "If you were a regular fee-charging lawyer, we might do business. But neither of us can survive on swamp gas."

He sighed. "It's my duty to come abruptly to the point, for your gentle consideration. In a nutshell, I propose matrimony. It is the one sure defense against the unjust fate that is gathering on the horizon. Now, that is certainly a remarkable proposition, coming out of the blue, but bear with me. By acquiring a husband, especially one who will act as a knight, you will be assured of safety and security."

"And you'll be assured of my mine."

"Ah, of course you would suppose that. But marriage is share and share alike. Your good fortune is my good fortune, and vice versa. In exchange for my interest in the mine, you would be stoutly defended against predators circling you like rabid wolves."

She was, actually, enjoying this.

"Now, about delicate things, madam. While you are the fairest flower of Edinburgh, and you make my heart and other organs quiver, I should be content with a marriage of convenience, at least until you discover in me the knightly qualities that might win your approbation."

"Do you like haggis?" she asked. "If not, your goose is cooked."

"I am not familiar with it, madam."

"Then your goose is cooked."

"Now, madam, there is more. If you should fail to welcome me to your bosom, there is always the possibility that my services might be employed by one or another of those who would like to find a shortcut to the McPhee gold. Now, I'm not saying I would succumb to such employment, but you see, the longer I wait, and the greater the distance between us, the larger the temptation."

"To circle me like a rabid wolf."

"Not I, madam, but my clients, who might use my considerable skills to find the wedge that will split your defenses wide open. Worse, if you employ that shotgun in some way not countenanced by law and civility, and it results in injury, you might face a court verdict that is many times what the McPhee Mine is worth. So all this takes some consideration."

"How many widows have you fleeced so far?" she asked.

"There is a dire shortage of widows in Montana Territory," he said. "You are a great rarity. This is a land of single males, many from abroad, who will send for their wives or sweethearts in due course. You are the true gold mine. Mineral is abundant in the territory, but a good, seasoned, experienced widow is pure bullion."

"I can think of other things that I'm pure of," she said.

He sighed, gently. "Now of course I understand perfectly how you must feel about me, about my proposal. A perfect stranger comes up the mountain proposing holy matrimony, and with an eye on your gold mine. Now hear this. I affirm it. My virtue is that I'm transparent. My every design is clear. That means you know the man you're dealing with, know what my plans are, and you won't have to deal with some secretive, silent, sly bamboozler full of nasty surprises. Here I am." He doffed his bowler and settled it gently over his dark hair. "Think about it," he said. "Scots thinkers are very superior."

"Horsepucky," she said.

"Would you mind if I meandered around a bit? I should like to see the mine that has become the object of my lusts," he said.

"And what are you going to do? Snatch some ore so you can have it assayed?"

"Not a bad idea," he said. "No, I thought I'd see if the corner cairns are properly in place, so that if you should turn me down I might have legal grounds to invalidate your claim under federal law. I fancy myself as a mine-robber."

"Why do I like you?" she asked. "Go right ahead."

"We're two of a kind," he said, clambering into the buggy. "Now, if I can urge this dray up that grade, I'll see the McPhee."

The buggy horse pushed into his collar and slowly dragged the buggy up the tough grade to the mine while she watched. She was entertained. Whatever else Hermes Apollo had done, he had given her a week's amusement.

She circled around through a forested slope until she could see what he was up to. He had parked the buggy and was hauling out some equipment, which she soon realized was a tripod and a bellows camera of the latest design. She watched him slide in a plate, adjust the lens, and then squeeze a bulb. He moved the tripod hither and yon, loading new plates into the big device. He photographed the mine head, the ore car, the rails, the shed, and then took some panoramic shots of the whole landscape. Then he loaded his equipment into the buggy, and eased down the hill.

By the time he reached the flat where she was camped, she was there again.

"Well, what did you discover?" she asked.

"I double as a mine broker, Mrs. McPhee. Say the word, and I'll put it on the market for, oh, half a million, but who knows whether I'll get it."

"What other professions do you own to?"

"Well, Hermes Apollo is an accountant, a lawyer, a geologist, a cartographer, a chemist, a professor, a divine, a journalist, and a linguist with a passing knowledge of French, Spanish, Greek, Mandarin, and Romany—gypsy, if I may say so."

"Are you a gypsy?"

"No, according to my mother I am half Greek god, half goat."

"What about the divine part of it?"

"Druid priest."

"Well, if nothing else works out, propose again and maybe I'll hitch up."

"Madam, you have run galvanic currents through me."

But she was smiling.

"What did you discover at the mine?" she asked.

"Madam, it is beyond words. Each day, when the late Kermit McPhee emerged from his brutal toil in that hole, he beheld the grandest prospect known to mortal eyes; vaulting slopes, peaks poking the clouds, noble mountains, lofty ridges and saddles, rushing creeks, and all of it painted by the hand of the divine. I stood there, contemplating this noble panorama, thinking that not all the gold in the bowels of that mine could equal the sheer pleasure of that vista. It was like dining at the table of the gods."

She liked that. He might be a mountebank, but he was a poetic one. And artful in hiding his intentions.

"I think maybe you're a mine broker along with the rest, Hermes Apollo. If you find a prospect, and he makes a fair offer, you'll get a commission."

"Oh, madam, I'm not interested in a mere commission. A small percentage? I've set my sights on grander goals, such as gathering the McPhee Mine and the widow McPhee to my bosom, and thus becoming the richest man on the planet."

"Get out of here before you take a load of buckshot."

He smiled broadly. "I count this trip a great success," he said.

"You would," she said. "For you, a quick trip to the outhouse is a success."

"You don't know the half of it," he replied.

"You want to do me a favor?"

"I leap at the chance," he said.

"I have some quartz ore I would like to deliver to the Drumlummon mill. It's such a small amount they may not want it, but I'd like to try. It's in a burlap bag. If you'd deliver it, that would be a valuable service. If they won't take it, I think the assayer will. He can reduce small amounts of quartz himself. Get a receipt from either one. Would you do it?"

"I'm flattered to think that you would give the mission to Hermes Apollo," he said. "The Greek god Hermes is the divine patron of travelers as well as the god of cunning, theft, commerce, and rascals. I am well named, you see. His Roman name is Mercury, fleetest of the gods, and in any gold mining town, mercury is known as the liquid that amalgamates with gold. Yes, entrust the quartz to your admirer and swain, Hermes Apollo, and watch what happens."

She found all this a little outlandish, but what did it matter?

"Wait," she said, and headed into the forest and caught up the heavy bag of ore. She dragged it toward his buggy.

"Permit me," he said, and lifted it into the ebony buggy.

"It does my heart good to sit in the vicinity of gold, whether in pure form or still caught in its ore. Putting that bag of ore into my buggy is like a wedding," he said.

"Except the gold is married to me," she replied.

He sighed. "And so it is," he said. "I'll have to marry you to marry the gold."

He lifted his well-brushed bowler from his oiled hair, settled it, and eased the weary horse into a fast walk down the long slope and into the gulch. She watched him diminish and then disappear. He worried her, actually. The man had a bag full of tricks.

She wondered if he was another of Constable Roach's minions, or one of that greedy clan, but she doubted it. She counted it as more pressure. Ever since Kermit's death, she had been subjected to pressure from nearly everyone she'd met. The funeral man, Laidlow, had pressured her, along with his hooligans; so had the city cop, Roach. So had this quack, who might or might not be a lawyer. But he was proving to be useful.

TEN

March was waiting at the assay office when Rolf Wittgenstein appeared.

He unlocked, smiled, and motioned her in.

"Early," he said. "What is your pleasure?"

He paused at the counter, as if listening to her were a duty to be performed. His flasks and furnaces needed his attention. She was struck again by the acrid odor of the place; whatever happened in laboratories was foreign to her.

"Do you buy or sell mining claims? Or broker mining properties?"

"Ah, I see what you're after. Now and then. But broker? No, there are gentlemen in the cities, like Helena, who do that. I take it you wish to sell the McPhee."

"I've needed to all along, but ever since Kermit . . . well, it's all I could do to keep strangers off."

"Gold does that. And you want me to find a buyer. A reputable buyer who will pay a proper price."

"That's why I'm here. You did the assays; you know more than anyone else what's there."

Wittgenstein could no longer contain his impulse to begin his ritual, and even as he talked he began building up charcoal fuel for his furnaces. She didn't mind. Oddly, it was easier for them to negotiate when he was busying himself.

"It's not really my business. A good broker could get you more, and has better contacts. But yes, I could—protect you. That I can be sure of. Now, I'll need to know some things. What do you expect of me?"

"A commission for a sale. I don't know how much. You know these things."

"And if I choose to become a partner in the mine, what of that?"

"You will find some way to protect me."

"And what if a buyer wants half a mine with you the other partner?"

"I would prefer an outright sale. Kermit told me the ways that partners are fleeced."

"They are too numerous to count, Mrs. McPhee." The assayer began pumping bellows, generating white heat in his assay furnace. "I trust you have Kermit's papers? The patent from the government?"

"No, that burned up."

"A copy of the application, the claim?"

"All that burned, sir."

"Did he leave a will?"

"Handwritten, everything to me, but it burned."

He abandoned his bellows for the moment. "That makes things difficult, but not impossible. You'll need to prove ownership if you hope to sell. But the government has its own records, and duplicates can be gotten. But that takes time."

"How much?"

"Bureaus are very slow, Mrs. McPhee. Let's say six months. And you'll need a lawyer to thread that needle."

"I might have one. If he's to be trusted."

That was all disheartening.

"Do you have a marriage license?"

"The parish record in Scotland."

"It would be a good idea to apply at once."

More delay. A wave of dismay swept March.

"I can't just sell the mine now?"

"Well, who'd buy it without the documents? Can you even prove it's yours?"

"What should I do?"

"Write for documents, find someone to mine it on shares while you wait, and never give up possession. Staying right there, on the property, would be the most important. But I'm no lawyer."

She thought of Apollo, and shrank from the idea of consulting him or employing him to achieve any of it. She wondered whether there might be another lawyer in Marysville who'd help.

Wittgenstein looked uncomfortable, and eager to begin his day's run of assays.

"Thank you," she said, and fled into the cold sun. She stood, blinking, in the glare of mountain light. Marysville had been thrown up swiftly, mostly from lumber that was scarcely cured. Its board-and-batten buildings leaked smoke from the stoves within. The smoke hung against the slopes, and would soon blow away when the breezes picked up. The thump of the Drumlummon stamp mill on the far side of town was the heartbeat of the place. When the thump of the mill stopped, so would Marysville. That's how it was with most mining towns. They came and went, swift shelter that would soon rot away in the winter snows and summer fires.

She drifted, aware of her shabby borrowed dress and ungroomed manner. But she lacked so much as a tin bathtub and soap. She was not just poor; she was swiftly running out of her last stores of vegetables and necessities in her root cellar. The clock was almost at midnight.

She passed Tipperary Leary's saloon, and saw it was dark. He opened at noon, he said. And that was a long time ahead.

But then the door burst wide, and there he was.

"It's a good thing I washed the window," he said. "It goes cloudy on me. Half my patrons smoke a pipeful each evening. If you don't mind stepping into a place not made for women, come in."

She did, still curious about saloons, and also glad to see his ruddy face and bold gaze, which was taking her in even as she plunged into the twilight of the interior.

He motioned her to a table, brought a jar of pickled eggs and another of pretzels, and asked what she might want to drink.

"Just . . . water, please."

"You look like you could use a good feast," he said. "We'll go over to the beanery and fill you up."

Somehow, that seemed the wrong thing to say, and she fell silent.

"There's more trouble, is there?" he asked.

"I can't hang on for long," she said. "And I have no place to go, and no vocation." She let the options remain unspoken. Women in her position arranged a swift marriage, easily done in the woman-shy west, or drifted into a life she didn't want to think about.

"The owner of a good mine? No place?"

"It will take time," she said. "Assuming that I'll ever get what I need."

She told him: No patent, no will, no evidence of marriage, no way to wait half a year—if that—for precious documents. No sale. And she without a roof over her head, and running out of food.

"And half the town, all the Roach clan, scheming to snatch it," Leary said. "You want to kiss it good-bye, or what?"

"I've had a marriage offer."

"Do my ears betray me? Marriage, you say. As in, nab the widow and the mine?"

"Yes."

"Some old billygoat, is he?"

"Yes."

"Would you keep my curiosity from burning a hole in the bar?"

"A lawyer named Hermes Apollo."

"The profane marrying the sacred, is it?"

"Which is which?" she asked.

He laughed. She nibbled on a pretzel, liking the salt. She liked being in a saloon. Life in saloons seemed to ooze possibility and hope and connection to the world. She liked being with Tip Leary, too.

"He drove up the lane to my mine, and introduced himself, and laid out some good reasons why we should marry, and as soon as possible. You seem to know him. What do you think?"

"I know him," Tip said, hesitating some.

She thought he was choosing his words carefully.

"A lot of show and posturing. The way he dresses, talks. But I hear things now and then. You want my half-baked and fool opinion about him? Underneath all that noisy surface is a man with a heart."

"Why do you say that?"

"It's a gift I have, to ken the heart."

"You know him well?"

"He's come in. And a barman hears things. I'm never without the word. I'll tell you a thing or two about Apollo. He puts his worst foot forward. Now, if he drove out there thinking to marry his

103

way into owning a gold mine, that was probably the way he started in with you. He probably said, March McPhee, you need a husband and I need a gold mine. And between us we'll lick the jackals."

She smiled. "It was a little like that. Yes, he does that. It's rather disarming, don't you see? And that's why I'm asking."

Tip Leary turned somber. "But that's not all I've kenned. Once he has his way with you, and gets you bound up in a marriage, it might not go so easy for you. The man's got a bag of tricks."

She nodded. "That's my fear. I'm a woman alone, and I am just edging my way along, not really knowing what to do. And now I see no way out. Marry Hermes Apollo, attorney at law, or walk away from the mine with nothing, scarcely even the borrowed dress you fetched me."

"Would you mind, madam, if I rallied some help for you?"

He sat there, looking almost like a supplicant rather than a rescuer. She hardly dared to speak.

"You need some help. You need to get those letters off, and you need to get yourself a cabin at your mine, and you need to get some ore out to pay for things. Here's what I'm thinking, Mrs. McPhee. I'll get some of the off-shift boys, most of them muckers in the Drumlummon, to go up the gulch and make things right. You'll need a little shack to call home for a bit. You'll need a little food to stay alive. You'll need some men who know how to blast and muck to bring out the ore and get it to the mill. You need some strong men who'll stand up to gangs trying to cop your mine. You'll need all that, and I think my patrons, most of them from the old country, will be glad to do it, and be glad to bust a few heads if it comes to it."

"You're describing a miracle."

"No, these boys were born poor, and born into a hard world, and they know what's mean and cruel in the human beast, and they'll take delight in keeping a new widow, husband killed in the pit by falling rock—yes, take a bit of pleasure helping out. Especially if I give them the word."

"Some day I'll repay. If they'd do that, and they can get some ore to the mill, most of the pay's theirs."

"Ah, don't worry your head about that, madam."

"But I must. It's an obligation."

"That's what's bonny in you. All right then. But there's one thing we can't help you with. Schemers will use the law and the courts and the police to rip your mine from you. You can count on it. There's not a man comes into my pub who knows how to deal with that, if it comes to it. The police have claws. Lawyers have claws. Courts have claws. You might just hire that man Apollo, for a fee of course, and my boys, they'll dig the ore to pay the lawyer to beat off the jackals."

"Mr. Leary, forgive me, but why are you doing this?"

"Justice, ma'am. I've seen injustice. Every man comes into my pub for some ale and a pipe has known injustice across the sea. That's why we're here, half a globe away from our home. We know about that, Mrs. McPhee. It's a memory bled into our bodies and our brains. The fight for justice never ends, never slows. And now that my patrons are here, in a new land, a free land, with none of the dead weight of the old world on their shoulders, they'll want to give a little back to this country, and maybe you'll be the way to do it."

She sat numbly in the twilight of the saloon, unable to summon words.

He vanished into his rear room and returned with a bundle.

"I thought you'd be needing a few things, and I've got a little stuff for you. There's a little clothing and dainties wrapped in here, and a little sack of rolled oats to keep body and soul together, and a bar of soap, and a few little things. Take it. I've been meaning to hike up there and leave it with you."

She took it gratefully. He ushered her into the sun and she started up the gulch to her mine, with the gift of hope.

ELEVEN

March paused in the mountain light of Marysville. She never grew weary of the ever-changing face of the mountains, as clouds bellied over them, or sun blazoned them, or sunset skies lit up behind them. She was far from her birthplace, but Marysville was home.

If she could keep it.

She hunted for the law office of Hermes Apollo, and was finally rewarded by a shingle dangling in the bright breeze, on a side street she had never traversed, a narrow lane close to the Drumlummon. There was an esquire after the name, and attorney at law beneath. The building was nondescript, but the door wasn't. It was lacquered ebony, and was a startling contrast to the roughly laid up shiplap of the structure.

She paused, collecting her courage and trying to anticipate his maneuvers, and then entered. Something, probably cowbells, jangled. There was no need for them. The single room housed the whole establishment, including Hermes Apollo in his shirtsleeves, the cuffs slightly soiled, a garter on his sleeve.

He plummeted upward and melted into an oleaginous smile.

"And so we meet again," he said. "Do you accept?"

"You might ask me to sit down," she said, and did without waiting.

"So I've lured you to my lair," he said. He was eyeing her in ways that made her uncomfortable.

Law books filled a glass-fronted case on one wall. Behind his enormous glossy desk was a portrait of a black-robed judge in wire-rimmed spectacles, a law book in hand.

"He's no relative," Apollo said. "But he's impressive, and intimidating, and well worth the twenty-seven dollars I paid for him in Altoona."

"Like your watch fob with the phi beta kappa key," she said.

"Cigar?" he asked.

She ignored him, and began the recitation: there was the problem of no patent, no will, no marriage record in the New World, and these would take months to acquire. And she could not hope to prove ownership or sell the mine without them. And she was under siege from all directions.

"It's a pickle," he said.

"Do you think you can apply for these things, fend off claim-jumpers, and help me sell the property when my ownership is established?"

"Wedlock, holy or unholy," he said.

"A marriage of convenience," she replied. "Not a hand will ever touch me."

"Wedlock, man and woman," he replied. "All

things shared and shared alike. Including you and the gold mine."

"Can you get the papers? Fend off Constable Roach, and his kin?"

"I am good at delaying the inevitable," he said, mysteriously.

"I am not inclined toward marriage. I have only just lost the man I've loved more than life. I'm sure you understand."

"Wedlock, whole and true," he replied. "That's what I treasure in you."

He certainly was cheerful. The rhythmic thump of the stamp mill up the slope reached her ears. Day by day, in Marysville, a fortune was being torn from the mountains.

"Justify it," she said sharply.

"A great endeavor. First, petition the federal land office for a fair copy of the patent. Send a request, indeed, duplicate requests to be on the safe side, to Edinburgh for the parish record. The will is less a problem. A wife inherits. But the mine is under siege. Word is that it will be seized for debt, or tax delinquency, or some such. They will invent these things faster than I can swat them down. In short, you are committing me to a lifetime vocation, for which I plan to be amply rewarded with the mine and March."

He was still standing, oddly forceful in his quietness.

"I cannot bear the thought of marriage. It's not

you, it's that I lost Kermit only a few days ago. I'm not ready."

He said nothing.

"If you succeed, get the papers here, fend off the people who want to cheat me out of it, restore it to me, and help either sell it or put it into operation, then—yes, take half ownership in the mine. But only then. Not now. As for marriage, I will do what I have to do. But only if you succeed in all else."

He reached into his humidor and pulled out a Havana and gave it to her.

"You win a cigar," he said.

"Was that a proposal?" she asked.

"It isn't a five-cent Baltimore stogie."

"It's the Hope Diamond of engagements," she said.

"The mail coach leaves at four for Helena. With a bit of scribbling, I can start matters rolling. The state mining bureau is only a few miles away."

"I'll want a contract," she said.

"Oh, an oral agreement will suffice, don't you know?"

"Write the terms, and if there's the slightest weasel in the wording, I won't sign."

He did. It was clear and unambiguous. She read it, reread it, and nodded. He made a fair copy. They each signed and dated the document, and she pocketed her copy. She walked into the daylight a betrothed woman—at least if he met all her terms.

There had been no parting handshake, much less a kiss, but a smile sufficed. She looked deep into his baggy eyes, and didn't recoil. He winked.

She was restored to the muddy streets of Helena a new woman. Or at least one with arrangements that affected every closet of her life. The day was benign. She had friends here.

She had no more business in town, and this was business enough for a long while. Three men. Three friends. Three allies. Mr. Wittgenstein, Mr. Leary, and Mr. Apollo. They had changed everything, simply because they wished to. She carried her little bundle, courtesy of Tip Leary, under her arm. His most precious gift was a ball of soap, which she would employ as soon as she could at the McPhee Mine. She saw Constable Roach down the street, and ducked into an alley, and managed to avoid the man at least for the moment.

But he was waiting for her when she rounded a corner.

"Good afternoon, Mrs. McPhee," he said. "I thought you should know that my office is now the whole of Marysville township, thirty-six square miles, which includes the various mining properties near town. I am the law there."

"Then you'll keep me safe," she said.

"The mine will be in good hands," he said. "I may deputize some officers."

He smelled of witch hazel, and his hair looked

newly trimmed. He was always natty. His blue uniform was spotless. He reminded her of a lordly passenger train conductor.

She edged around him and soon was treading up the wide gulch out of town. She felt his eyes on her back, but it was only her imagination.

For some reason the hike from town up to the mine was wearisome, and she toiled through the second mile, suddenly exhausted. She had accomplished all she could that day, hadn't she? Then, when she rounded the bend, and saw the ash-heap that had been her home, and her rude camp nearby, and the few things she had salvaged, a great wave of sadness engulfed her.

What had she done? What madness had got ahold of her? Kermit was barely in his grave, her boy had been lost to fire only a few days before, but here she was, committed on paper to marry someone she didn't know, someone who repelled more than warmed her. She had set aside every caution, written her signature on a paper that would change her life, and for what? For just what?

Even if Mr. Apollo was a good man, she felt nothing for him. Even if he got her papers together and rescued the mine and gave her a comfortable life, what good was it? Did she care for him? Love him? No, it was a fear of loss, of a mine, of her independence, of support, of respectability that had driven her. Fear, not love. Desperation, not desire. She felt her weariness steal through her limbs, robbing energy from them until she could barely walk. She passed by the ashes, reached her camp, and fell to the ground, desolated by the mistakes she had made this day, and by her own foolishness. Or stubbornness. Or maybe even her own greed.

She sensed she would regret this day the rest of her life. She sat bleakly beside her few things, until at last she undid Tip Leary's bundle, and beheld a soft gray woolen dress, needed warmth even in a Montana summer, and the small sack of oats, and the ball of home-made soap. The soap filled her with a longing so great she had no words for it. After days of living barely washed and never clean, she could clean herself.

She found kindling and wood and started a fire in the stove, which sat nakedly on the earth. She started water heating in the tin kettle. She rinsed the ash out of the sheet metal tub. She fetched more water in the wooden bucket, and as soon as the first pailful was hot, she poured it into the tub and started more warming. Nervously, she eyed the trail winding far below. She would see anyone ascending it long before they saw her, and that was all she needed. And yet it felt strange, and intimidating, to bathe in open air.

She fetched the soap, holding it as if it were gold, and when she at last had enough warm water, she stepped in, and luxuriated in it, and then scrubbed herself, lathering soap over her, cleaning her flesh, even if she could not clean away the darkness she felt about signing that paper committing her life and fortune to that man, that Hermes Apollo, names she could barely conjure up, and names that filled her with bleakness. What had the lawyer offered except some security and imprisonment in a cold marriage? How different that was from Tip Leary's tender gift, the soap, the warm dress, the promise of help to rebuild. Tip had given her gifts; Hermes Apollo had only offered a deal, a vast return on a small service. Tip Leary had a heart. Hermes Apollo had only an eye for easy pickings.

But in time, the warm water and suds did their magic, and about the time the water turned chill, she emerged, dried and dressed herself, and felt herself to be a woman once again. But the sadness stayed on. She had made a dreadful mistake, and had bound her life away.

She slipped into the soft gray dress Tip had given her. Nothing could have felt better. Scots knew wool, lived in wool, cherished wool, and now this wool warmed not only her body but her heart. She felt Tip's presence there, a friendship that had grown simply out of Tip's charity.

She knew she had to undo what she had done this day. She examined the paper, the simple contract that bound her perhaps for the rest of her life, if he made good his end of the bargain.

She stared at her own signature, scarcely believing she had willfully written it, willfully bargained her life away.

Her thoughts drifted to Kermit, and she sensed his presence there in the wilderness camp they had called home for so little time. What would he want her to do? She decided that was the wrong question. What should she do to make his quest to give her a good life become reality?

She found a sunlit spot where she could let wind and sun dry her hair, and there she sat weighing her future. And there, while breezes toyed with her glossy red hair, she decided that she would not pursue any future; she would let the future come to her. Things had been set in motion. Tip was sending his patrons to build a new cabin, begin mining gold, and keep her safe, and all for the pleasure of doing it. And Mr. Apollo would, or wouldn't, get the papers together, protect her from predators, and keep her safe from people with warrants and summons and judgments. She was not alone.

TWELVE

At first light, March awakened to the rattle of a wagon, and hastily clad herself. A group of working men in brogans and worn britches were toiling up the grade, along with a mule-drawn wagon loaded with something. It was barely five, but the nights were short in June.

She collected her shotgun and went to the road to meet them, her pulse rising.

They halted, aware of the weapon in her arms.

"The widow McPhee is it?"

She nodded.

"Himself, Tip Leary, sent us," said a burly one with carrot hair. "We're all on the second shift at the Drumlummon, but we're here to do a little fixing for you, if it's a thing you need. Before we go into the pit."

"Oh, my, you are welcome," she said. "You and Mister Leary are most kind to me. Whatever it is, go right ahead."

"It's a pride in us to help. Is it your husband was lost to a collapse here?" He didn't wait for a reply. "We can't save him, but we can save others. We've some timber men and some muckers, and we've some canvas and a little stovepipe and all. You show us where you'd like the little house put up, and we'll do it."

"A house, you'd do that?"

"A wall tent on a pole frame, then. We'll get some poles up, make a frame, hang the canvas, get your stove in with the fitting to take the pipe through the roof. And these lads here, Micks every one, they'll cut some lodgepole and put a square set or two into the shaft, brace up that bad spot where the rock's hanging and ready to take the life of anyone in that hole."

"I am March McPhee, and you are?"

They were content with first names: Two Mikes, a Harry, Sean, Peter, Ambrose, Brian, Kenneth, and two Dans. The red-haired one was a Dan.

"I will make sure that you are repaid," she said.

Dan shook his head. "Not a man here would allow it," he said. "Some of us would leave a widow behind; some not. But we who go into the pits, we're all brothers."

Somehow or other, they all felt a solidarity with Kermit, with the lost baby, and her. She wondered at it.

They swiftly spread out, several heading for the mine, others to a thicket of young lodgepole pines where the trees crowded together. They plucked up axes and saws and tools she scarcely knew, and began hacking down the lodgepoles and limbing them. Others tackled thicker trees, limbed them, and began snaking them up the grade to the mine, where they would soon become mining timbers. She watched amazed. The pole frame of a cabin rose swiftly, not far from the ashes of her home and life. A ridgepole and rafters were lashed down, and then the canvas was wrapped around the poles and laced into place until there were four taut walls, one with a door opening, and a taut cover. A golden light filtered through the cloth, making the interior glow. In the space of a few hours, these busy and artful men erected a solid shelter against weather, one that even had a wooden floor made from Kermit's stores at the mine head.

They had a sheet metal fitting that would keep the stovepipe heat away from the canvas, and two of these men soon had it anchored and the stove ready for use.

They stood silently while she inspected her new shelter, the glowing room, the floor, the release from chill air, the safety of a small home.

"It'll take you through the summer and into the fall," Dan said. "After that, you'll want to come live in town, I'm thinking."

They smiled when she thanked them, and seemed eager to get on with whatever else they had in mind, which was timbering the mine.

There, a crew of four sawed and notched the stout lodgepole trunks into a square set timbering of the dangerous area of the shaft, wedged the timbers in place, and slid lagging, or ceiling poles, into place above the crossbeams. The fractured rock was held at bay with a wooden cube jammed tight and ready to fend off most any collapse in the roof of the shaft. They were experienced timber men, used to erecting stout bulwarks and timbers deep in the Drumlummon, and knew exactly what they were doing.

Then Dan showed her the timbering by the light of a carbide lamp.

"I should like to know who you are, and how I may be your friend," she said to Dan.

"Oh, we're just patrons of our friend Tip. And he's not getting off for free. He promised us a spare mug for it. So you see? It's not for nothing we're working here."

"Just you wait!" she said. "I'll get even with you!"

The whole lot were grinning.

"We're on the moonlight shift, four to midnight, and it's time for us to go down the hill," said Dan. "You'll see some more of us. Some powdermen, they'll set up a little charge at the head, and some muckers, they'll clean it out and put the quartz in an ore car. But that's not for today."

"What do they pay you at the Drumlummon?" she asked.

"Three a day, and some of us get more."

"Then you'll get that, too."

Dan sighed. "Ma'am, don't take the brother out of it, please. It's not only for you. It's for him that you lost here, going into the shaft and not coming out."

Some sort of brotherhood, then.

"So we put up good timbers in his memory."

Then they were gone. If they hurried, they would meet the whistle at four. And put in another long shift before they saw their beds. She felt an odd loneliness as she watched them hurry their mule and wagon down the slope to the gulch, and then vanish. It was past three in the afternoon, but the day had transformed her life. Now, suddenly, she had a safe mine, a shelter, and hope. And she barely knew their names. Friends of Tipperary Leary; that was all.

She arranged her few possessions in her snug shelter but her mind wasn't on the task. She was safe from most weather, but that wasn't in her thoughts. She could survive the long wait for the papers, but that didn't occupy her. No, the visit from Tip Leary's saloon patrons had brought something else to her attention. They had not come to help or console a new widow out of luck, though that had been present. They had not come to share her new and sharp grief. They had not come especially for her, a woman in trouble. They had come to honor a bond they felt with any man who braved the pits. Any man, anywhere, Hibernian or not, who gathered his courage and plunged into the bowels of the earth for a long shift with the sun hidden from his eyes and soul. In a way, they had come to pay homage to Kermit.

Was this brotherhood among men the same as

sisterhood she often felt toward her own sex? She could not say, and maybe it wasn't important. Strangers had honored Kermit McPhee and looked to his widow and his property. It all seemed a mystery to her; she, a new and hurting widow, and Dan, their spokesman, looking beyond her, his every word respectful, and yet serving a male brotherhood.

She wondered whether Kermit would have fathomed all this. It left her oddly pained, but so did most everything these dark times.

That evening she found herself entertaining a visitor. She discovered Constable Roach slowly climbing the grade to her shelter and mine. He walked easily, a compact man in fine condition, wearing his natty blue uniform. He was carrying a folder or envelope of some sort. A small silver bar pinned to his lapel identified him as the village peace officer. She debated whether to collect her shotgun, and decided against it. He stood on the small flat, eyeing the ashes of what had been her home, her new shelter, the woods beyond, and finally her.

"Good evening, Constable," she said.

He took that for permission to come close, surveying her all the while with those spaniel eyes. "Here's something for you," he said, and handed her the envelope.

She took it.

"There, then. That's a summons and you've

been served properly. Your presence is required in district court."

"For what?"

"Collection of debt, as I understand it. You owe the Laidlow Funeral Home a sum. They've gone to court. This action requires you to pay in ten days, that's tomorrow, or the mine will be attached. I should add that there's a court order prohibiting the removal of anything of value, such as ore, which might reduce the value or prevent my brother-in-law from full satisfaction."

"What court?"

"The territorial district court in Helena. My cousin, Samuel Roach, presides there."

"I see."

"I'm glad you do. We are a tight-knit family, each branch of which looks after the advancement and well-being of the rest."

"And how much time have I, and what happens if I fail to raise the funds?"

"You'll want to be there tomorrow. The mine will be attached and sold to satisfy the debt unless you bring cash."

"And once the mine is sold, do I get the balance, beyond what is owed for Kermit's funeral?"

"I don't imagine you will. There's no evidence that you own it. It belonged to your paramour."

"Paramour?"

He smiled slightly. "Can you prove otherwise?"

"Then why issue a summons to me?"

"You contracted the funeral services." He discovered a stump and sat on it. "I'll take some tea and enjoy the sunset with you," he said. "Nice prospect here, the view down the gulch."

Maybe that was a good idea. She headed wordlessly to her shelter, where some hot water rested on the stove, and prepared the Earl Grey for him, and for herself.

"I have no sugar."

"Tea has its own manly flavor," he said. "Nobler than coffee."

She handed him a crockery cup of it, and kept another for herself. Those were the sum of her crockery.

"So what happens if the mine is sold? Is there bidding?"

"My cousin will make sure there's an appearance of it."

"Which means, I suppose, that one or another of your clan will snatch my mine for a song."

He shrugged. "That's probably all it's worth. An exploratory hole is hardly a bonanza. We thought we'd take the risk. We may end up losing our shirts. But it's all under way, and there's no way you can derail it."

"Except to pay the undertaker."

"Oh, there are other approaches if you do that. A considerable amount of tax money is overdue on this place, you know. We discovered it recently. The court can seize it, you know. And there's some question about the patent; whether it is valid. There may have been an earlier claim on this very ledge." He sipped. "Earl Grey. My favorite, and well brewed. You have gifts, Mrs. McPhee, or is that the right title?"

"It is the right one."

"Well, I'm glad of that. One of my duties is to look after the morals of the village of Marysville. Thomas Cruse, owner of the Drumlummon, would have no other. We have none of the wickedness of Helena here."

She reddened, furious, but choked it down. He was observing her closely, well aware of her gust of rage.

"Nice fellows, the ones from Leary's saloon, coming up here to build you a shelter. I gather they timbered that bad patch in the mine, too. That adds to the value, and that will help us ascertain what sort of operation Kermit McPhee was running. But that was generous of them, and I'm sure you'll be returning the favor any way you can."

She threw her cup at him. It splashed by, barely wetting him. He stood abruptly, amused.

"Time to head down the hill, my lovely friend. It wouldn't be seemly for the town constable to be seen with the merry widow after dark."

He lifted his visored cap and headed his natty way down the trail.

THIRTEEN

The pair stood outside her shelter in the dawn light, along with a laden mule. They had awakened her. She peered out, discovering the skinniest men she had ever seen.

"Friends of Tip," one said.

"Powdermen," said the other.

"We'll drill, put in some sticks, and blast. Tomorrow, there'll be muckers."

She was getting the idea. The slope was soaked in predawn gray, and a deep hush lay over the mountainside. These two were so thin she couldn't imagine them doing heavy labor. But they were wiry, and muscles lumped out of their arms.

She needed to think about this. There was that paper that forbade it.

"I don't think I'm allowed," she said.

"Tip Leary said go ahead, don't worry about nothing. They can't stop us."

It was a hard decision to make. She still felt sleep-fogged. The mule twitched restlessly. The packs were heavy, and sagged.

"I'm Del and this is Will," said one. "We're doublejackers."

"I guess I don't know."

"Tip says they're trying to push you out, and it's the Laidlow crowd, so nothing's fair and right,"

125

said Will. "They don't even need to know about it. You need a little ore? You'll have some ore."

She was fully awake now. "What will you do?"

"We've got steels; I hold and turn the steel while he hammers, then he holds and turns the steels while I hammer. Each steel's a tiny bit narrower than the previous. When we get the holes drilled and cleaned, then we crimp Bickford into the caps, cut the caps into the DuPont sticks, slide the sticks into the face, and when we're ready we ignite the rat tails a certain way and get out of there. There'll be a thumpety-thump, and that's it. Maybe three feet of rock and ore to muck out. All quiet as a church on a Monday night."

"I've watched my husband do it," she said.

"Then the muckers come, but that's tomorrow, long before dawn, and they'll clean the load out before anyone's awake," said Del. "There isn't nobody gonna know the shaft runs three feet farther, and you've got some quartz for the mill."

Something in it froze up in her.

"The court says I can't remove ore," she said.

"The court belongs to them that wants to drive you off," Del replied.

She stared into the predawn gray, uncertain.

"There's something in me that respects the law," she said. "Whether or not it's just. Thank you for coming. I'll see what the day brings."

"We've hiked a long way, ma'am."

"I know that, and I'll make it good somehow."

"You're letting yourself be run down like a fox," Del said. "They have the hounds."

"I know," she said.

"Tip, he won't be happy."

"Tip is the kindest man I've met. Thank him for me."

"You mind if we stash this stuff near the mine?"

"There's nothing against it," she said.

"We'll find a place out of the way. It'll be handy."

She nodded. She'd rarely felt such a heaviness. It was as if she had thrown hope and success out the window. She watched them lead the mule up the mine trail and then disappear above. She returned to her shelter, feeling foolish, and spent an uneasy hour preparing for the day. She neither heard nor saw the powdermen and the mule retreat to the gulch. She thought that if Constable Roach heard about it, he'd be amused. The man was often amused, usually by the foolishness of others.

Why had she sent them away? She couldn't say. They had offered to help her, to toil hard for hours, to expose themselves to danger, to dig her out of her troubles. They and the muckers who would shovel out the rock the following day. They and Tip Leary, shepherding her against impossible odds. And yet for some unfathomable reason she had chosen to heed the injunction of a biased court. She couldn't explain her conduct to herself, and finally decided she was stubborn, a trait she knew a lot about, because every Scot she knew was stubborn, including Kermit. It flashed through her thoughts that she was being honorable, but that was silly. There is no honor in heeding the dictates of a judge looking after his relatives.

The heaviness stayed with her. It was upon her when two more men toiled up the grade, but these two she knew. They were Jerusalem Jones and Bum Carp, part of Roach's little army, lackeys for the funeral home. Fear laced through her. She raced to her shelter and got the shotgun, and met them as they approached the forlorn flat, with its ash heap, and the canvas house built by Tim Leary's friends.

They stared across a chasm, not in the earth but dividing the soul. She knew them better than they knew her.

"Hey, put that thing down, lady," Jerusalem said. "We've been deputized. We're township constables, old Roach pinned on the badges, and if you wave that shotgun at us, and threaten peace officers, you're gonna regret it."

"You have no right to be here."

He grinned. "We're moving in. Court says, you can't take anything of value out, and we're gonna see to it. Just keeping it honest, you see? You try to make off with property, like gold ore, that's being contested in court, you'll end up rattling bars in a cage for a couple of years. Get it?"

"Get off my property. If that's what's bothering you, camp in the gulch."

"Naw. We thought we'd camp right there in that nice tent. Looks about right, don't it, Bum?"

"This is my home. You'll not stay here."

"Looks like we've got us a domestic to keep us tidy during our stay," Jerusalem said.

"Camp up at the mine if you must. That's what you want anyway."

"No, you got things of value you might make off with, like that shotgun. That could help pay debts, I think."

They both wore sidearms. But neither was in any sort of uniform.

"We saw a couple of miners and a mule on the road. You know anything about them?" Bum asked.

"I wouldn't tell you if I did."

They eyed each other. "Bum, go up and see if they've been messing with the mine."

Bum trotted up the sharp slope to the mine head while March and her captor waited in silence. Some puffball clouds scraped distant peaks. When Bum returned he seemed agitated.

"They're fixing to do it. They got timbering in there, ready for some serious digging. But the face wasn't touched."

Jerusalem grinned. "Seems like we got here just in time to prevent illegal stuff going on." He turned to March. "You gonna stay here and cook for us and clean the outhouse?"

She saw how it would be.

"Leave that here," Jerusalem said, nodding at the shotgun.

"You will not enter my home," she said, and stood squarely in the doorway through the canvas.

"You call that a home?" Jerusalem said. "Canvas on poles?"

"You burnt my home," she said. "You won't burn this one."

They grinned. "What are you talking about? Burnt your home? Are you resisting arrest or something?"

"Did you burn it?"

"What home?" Bum asked.

That was answer enough.

"Out!" she yelled, lifting the shotgun.

They rushed her, knocked her down, yanked the shotgun, pinned her down. She writhed and bucked, but there was Jerusalem, holding her to the earth.

He let loose of her and stood.

"You've got two choices. Either you walk out of here on your own, now, or we'll walk you out, straight to the lockup in town, and charge you. Threatening a peace officer, that should keep you in irons."

She clambered to her feet and walked away, their eyes following her as she made her way down the grade and into the gulch. She doubted she would ever see her property again. And in a little while, the clan would own the mine. And if she lingered in Marysville, they would find some way to harass or shame her.

It was a long, weary walk. She did not plunge directly into Marysville, but skirted it to the small green cemetery where Kermit lay, and sat quietly beside the raw earth that covered him.

"Have to say good-bye now, Kermit. You left me a good mine, and it's gone," she said. "You and I brought a good child into the world, and he's gone," she said. "And you and I, we made a good match, and you're gone. I still have life and memories."

She sat in the morning quiet a while, remembering her man, remembering the comfort of his arms. And then it was time to go.

She drifted toward Hermes Apollo's office near the big mine, walked in, found him alone. He peered up from his desk, where he had been perusing a law book. He seemed less flamboyant there, except for the gaudy sleeve garter.

"I need the cash. From the ore you took to the mill," she said, abruptly.

He sighed. "Actually, you owe them thirty-seven dollars. The batch was so small it cost them more to mill it than you got out of it."

"How much gold in it?"

"Two and a half ounces. Fifty dollars refined, but milled gold has some impurities. Worth about seventeen an ounce. Now tell me the rest."

"I've been driven out," she said. "By the hooligans. The ones with the funeral home. The ones who burnt down my cabin. Jerusalem Jones and Bum Carp."

She told him that story, and then told him about the earlier visit from two powdermen ready to do some blasting. And after a moment, she confessed:

"I wouldn't let them. I suppose that was dumb."

"Why wouldn't you let them?"

"The court order."

She had to tell him about that, too. He hadn't heard.

"I'll retract my offer to marry you," he said. "I wanted the gold mine, and now it's gone."

She hadn't expected to laugh, but she did.

"But you could live in sin if you'd like," he said.

"I may take you up on it, but not yet."

"Meaning you'll go dicker with the barkeep first. Let me see what's to be done here. The Helena court's a half day away, and there's not much I can do against the local constabulary. But we could always elope."

He was making a joke of it. That was the trouble with the gasbag. She whirled out, into the glare of midday sun, and headed for the saloon hoping Tip Leary would be about. He wasn't. She was alone. It hit her hard. She would soon need food. And shelter. And something to wear. She could wait for Tip and beg for help. She could find some of those miners, now off-shift, and beg for help. Or she could fight, and maybe die trying if it came down to that.

There was the overhang on the slope off a ways from the mine boundary. There was the root cellar, which she could reach furtively, at night. There was Kermit's shirt and pants and boots at the overhang. There was Kermit's own explosives stashed near the mine head. There was the stash of those powdermen, somewhere.

She might have found a welcome in town. Walk into any church and get help. Marry some male on the spot; she knew there were scores of lonely miners ready to tie the knot. But that was not to be. She turned her back on Marysville. Instead, she walked wearily up the familiar gulch, with its walls of anonymous dark forest climbing the slopes. She cut off at a familiar spot, and worked through brush, past a bear nesting ground, past a dripping spring, ever higher, until she reached the place where native rock broke out in jagged strata, and a few minutes more took her to the overhang, not far from her mining claim. This would be home. It would umbrella her. With a little effort she could add to its comfort, barricade the wind and weather.

Kermit's britches and shirt were where she had left them. She climbed into them, again discovering the comfort of flannel and the odd liberation of pants. Even rolled-up pants. The next step was to steal food and maybe a blanket or some sort of cover. And after that, to fight her guerrilla war bare-handed and never quit and never surrender.

She was now as feral as a bitch wolf.

FOURTEEN

March McPhee discovered she had no trouble living in the wild. She found wild strawberries, as tiny as her fingernail, carpeting some hollows, and huckleberries, too. She smuggled potatoes and onions from her own root cellar, and even slipped into her canvas house to nab her clothing and blankets when no one was there. She collected her shovel and pick and hammer, and hauled them to her redoubt. These she used to build rock walls that effectively shielded her from the occasional mountain storm.

She ached now and then to slip into Marysville, but that would serve no purpose. There was nothing her friends could do for her. Tip Leary's miners had tried again to work the mine, but Roach's thugs had driven them off at gunpoint, and after that all forays into the property ceased. All this she had watched from several vantage points that enabled her to look down upon the mine head, and even the canvas house below. There wasn't much that escaped her.

She felt free, most of the time, to wander the area of the mine head, picking up valuable items. One day she discovered a cache of explosives, DuPont powder, copper caps, Bickford fuse, plus some equipment, too, such as a crimper, an acetylene lamp, and a box of kitchen matches. All these things vanished from the mine, and were stowed strategically and safely in or near her redoubt.

The summer days and nights passed one by one. No doubt things were happening. Courts were issuing edicts. Property was being seized. Plans being laid to start the mine up, this time for its alleged new owners, known as the Roach Clan, or sometimes the Laidlow Group, but encompassing several families.

March continued to ghost around the property, noting exactly when its watchmen departed, as they occasionally did. And then she slipped in, pillaged the canvas cabin, and made off with even more items. A blanket, a cook pot, a fork and spoon. She always took care not to call attention to herself, and with each passing day learned how to glide through the dense forest, leave no mark of her presence, live off the land, and keep a watch over the mine.

The watchmen were bored and restless. One day she spotted them at the mine head. One was standing guard while the other was deep within. When at last he emerged, he was carrying a heavy burlap sack. So they were nipping ore themselves, no matter what the court's edict might be, and in defiance of their employer, Uncle Mortimer Laidlow. That was the beginning. Soon they were gold-fevered, and spending more and more time at the mine head. They avoided any blasting, but managed to chisel and hammer ore out of the quartz seam. That would soon come to an end, though. The day would come when they could no longer sledge out quartz. The seam was narrow and surrounded by country rock that had to be blasted loose.

They must live somewhere in Marysville, and next time one of them walked into town she intended to shadow him. She was gradually thinking up some things she might do to make their long stay at her mine less comfortable. She was tempted to burn the canvas shelter, but that would only trigger a major manhunt for her. No, she would remain invisible if she could, and for as long as she could manage.

She didn't know what she'd do when winter set in, but that was months away, and maybe she'd have her mine back by then. But that looked less and less probable to her. Loneliness dogged her. She starved for company, and was often tempted to slip into town just to talk to someone, anyone, such as Tip Leary. But for some reason she didn't. She could not explain herself. She was becoming a hermit, even against her better judgment.

One day Jerusalem Jones headed into Marysville toting a heavy sack, no doubt full of her ore. She shadowed him, knowing how to be invisible, always on the slopes, never on the trail or the bottoms. He grew wary in town, paused whenever he saw anyone, and finally delivered the ore to the assayer. So, maybe this was just another assay. But she remembered that the assayer was capable of refining small quantities—for a price. Jones emerged in a while, without the sack of ore, and headed for the Laidlow Funeral Home, and disappeared there. She hesitated to follow him there, on a busy street, wearing Kermit's britches and shirt, which would have scandalized anyone who saw her. So she retreated until twilight fell and she could move stealthily. She hoped to find some sign of Jones, but he had vanished.

She had evolved a way of ghosting straight through Marysville, using doorways, shadows, alleys, hedges, and now she eyed the city hall and its constabulary office. A single lamp burned in a window. Roach was nowhere to be found. She located him at Mac's Eats, where he was dining importantly. She slipped into his sanctum and studied it. There were shotguns in a rack on the wall, and she was tempted to take one to replace the one stolen from her. But she didn't. She noted the ease with which the office was breached. The constable was scarcely worried about crime in the village. She spotted a key ring, and tried the key in the cell lock, and found it threw the bolt. She returned the key ring, and looked for another, which she found in a desk drawer. She felt bad about snooping. The town was quiet, and she felt she was violating its peace, just by poking around the empty constabulary.

She yearned to talk to Tip Leary, but that would place her there, and she decided against it. She slipped into the fullness of night, pausing at shadowed doors to make sure the coast was clear. Marysville was sleepy; Constable Roach had little more to do than keep rowdy boys from tormenting dogs.

She watched him finish his meal at the restaurant, leave without paying, and amble along the street, trying the doors of businesses without scaring up an army of thugs. When he reached the brightly lit funeral home, he turned in, and she saw him welcomed there by his brother-in-law, and saw several others, all male, through the window. She edged closer hoping to hear, since it was summer and most of the sash windows in Marysville were opened wide to catch any stray breeze. But she couldn't make out the conversation. One of those present was Jerusalem Jones, and she wondered whether he told them about taking ore samples to the assayer. Maybe he had been asked to do just that; then again, she doubted it.

Jones left, started through pale moonlight toward the mine, and she shadowed him all the way. He was unsuspecting, and never turned to see who or what might be coming along behind a hundred yards or so. He reached the grade leading to the McPhee, climbed it, and entered the canvas shelter. She edged around to the rear, glad there were no dogs, and listened to Jones and Carp. It proved to be easy. The canvas obscured nothing but herself, there in the dark.

"Court's seized the mine; we're pretty much through here. There's no fight. The woman's gone. Soon as the boss gets it, he'll be digging ore. If we're going to do it, we'd better set to work. You game?" Jones asked.

"Ah, they'll need a few days to hire a crew, and even then they'll fool around, getting equipment."

"Naw, they'll move fast."

"What did the assayer say?"

"Well, that's not so good. He pulled out some quartz, put on his spectacles, and studied it some. From the McPhee Mine? That's what he asked. I didn't want to say, so he pulled out a pad of forms. Sign the form, sez he. So I study on the form, and it authorizes him to do an assay and take a fee for it, and it sez the signer is owner or authorized agent, and he stares at me. I sez, I'll check with the owner, and hold off. So he nods, and the ore's in there waiting for a signature on a form, and I am thinking maybe putting my name on the line, that's just asking for it, not so much because of the woman but because of the family."

"So it's just sitting there? Could we take it to the mill for a custom milling?"

"Beats me. We'd need a lot more ore to make a full load for custom milling."

"Not much time for that—unless we start now."

"I'm tired. I've walked all day. Took twenty, thirty pounds of ore down there. And now you want to go dig a ton out."

"You got any better idea?"

She didn't hear the answer. The man probably just shook his head.

"If we don't get it now, someone else will. And we'll lose our only chance," Bum said. "It don't matter if you're halfway worn out. Nothing matters but digging it out while we can. We'll put in a hard night, for sure, but it's worth it. You and me, we'll run a ton through the mill down there, and we'll put enough in our britches to live like kings."

"For a while, Bum, and then what?"

"We're part of the clan. We'll get our cut. That's what old Laidlow himself said. Everyone in the clan gets a share."

"Let someone else mine it. We'll get our cut," Jerusalem said.

"Sure, one twelfth of the profits."

"Less, last I counted."

"Well, that's my point. Get it now and it's ours. Get that lamp. Get a pick or two and a shovel and some sacks. You can sleep tomorrow; tonight we're getting ours."

So the pair was looking to clean out some of her ore, ahead of the Roach takeover.

Gold did strange things to people, even pitting one family member against another.

So they had been stealing—and hiding it. She slipped into the darkness of the forest, wondering what to do, if anything. When she reached her redoubt under the overhang, she sat down, almost as weary as Jerusalem Jones.

She built a fire in her hidden vale and brewed bitter tea, and stared into the eve, gaining no wisdom. She felt helpless against them. Those who wore pants seemed to own a power that she lacked.

She thought of Scotland. Was there any Scot not familiar with death? It visited all too often, and plucked the young away. What else did the poet write about? Robert Burns wrote of death, and sometimes love, but mostly death.

She had wanted only to bring love to the table: to hold her wee one on her knee and slide a bit of porridge into him, and watch him grow strong and supple, and become the man her husband had always been. That was a woman's role, but also her fate. The good and the bad, like the time she had nursed Fourth through milk fever, and he lived. But here she was, wearing Kermit's britches, alone, and cast into the wilderness, and losing what little he had left her.

She scarcely knew how to defend herself, she who wished to be as fragrant as the heather on the hill, and as pleasing to the eye. She whose dream was a nesting one, supple and happy in the compass of her husband's world. But this wasn't Scotland, and she had no husband to please and to protect her and his wee ones.

There was a task awaiting her, an obligation wrought from blood, and not anything she would have chosen to shape her life. She shied from it. Defend herself, yes, if she could. That could be a woman's work. But war, that was farther away than her inner eye could see. Could she hurt them, the ones who pillaged and burned? Could she return war when she should sue for peace? And was she made of the same stuff as a man, as hard and determined to fight as whatever lay in a man, which seemed to rise from his very stones?

She felt a certain inevitability. Not that she called, not that she chose the vocation of war, but that it came upon her and she could not avoid it. It was not her calling, fighting a war. It was something that had landed on her as hard as the slab of rock had landed on Kermit and snuffed his life. She would do what she must, but never again call herself a woman, or dream of holding her own wee babe at her breast.

She had no weapons, but what did it matter? She would use what came to hand. She had neither sword nor firearm, but she had an iron will, forged by cruelty. And the more she thought about war, the more she understood how to wage it. In fact, this very night might be a good time to begin.

Farther along the cliff, under the same overhang, she had stored Kermit's mining supplies, along with those cached by the two powdermen. She hoped she knew how to put them to good use.

FIFTEEN

The pair of them were feverishly hacking quartz ore from her mine, and she could see faint light from their acetylene lamp at the portal. Once in a while she heard clatter, the sound of rock landing in Kermit's old one-ton ore car.

The night lay still and quiet, with scarcely a breeze. The milky way lay as a powdery streak across the heavens, tens of thousands of sparkles, like a field of dreams, showing mortals the edges of infinity. She smelled the pine, which had baked in the summer sun, and now leaked aromatic scents on the playful night breezes. The slopes were thick with lodgepole, Douglas fir, spruce, as well as groves of bright aspen. She had always felt she was in some sort of earthly version of heaven. She thought maybe God had created mountains to show himself to mortals.

It was July, and warm, one of the few warm nights she had experienced in the high country. She would have been happy this eve holding Kermit Four in the chair on her porch, with her husband beside her, the three of them a small family making its way in the Territory.

But these two, back in that slightly inclined shaft, were stealing her ore, her substance, her very life. She could even see them, moving shadows light dancing off their shovels and picks, as they toiled.

There they were, betraying their relatives, working feverishly to get the gold before anyone else did. There they were, the pair who had tried to shut down her mine, burned her home, took the life of her son, and left her homeless. There they were.

She would bury them there. She hastened through the forest, over the low ridge, to her hideaway, began collecting the things she would need to turn her mine into a tomb. She lit a candle lamp so she could see what she was doing. She got a copper-sheathed cap, treacherous to handle. She got the fuse, the crimping tool, and half a dozen waxy red sticks of DuPont dynamite. She got some wire that would bind her bomb together. She got her knife, so she could insert the fuse into a stick.

She started in, slicing three feet of fuse, slipping it into the cap and crimping it, and then she began building her bomb. And all the while, her mind was fevered with the thought of trapping them there, at the back of her little mine, turning it into their tomb. And if their relatives ever dug them out, they would see betrayal along with death.

But there was something else working in her mind, the thought of birds singing their heart out at the dawn of a fine summer's day. And then she set down her tools and stared into the night. She was a woman meant to nurture life, not destroy it. They might deserve to die, but she was not the one who would release the guillotine blade. She stood, peered out at the stars, and knew she could not do it. She could fight them tooth and nail; she could not simply kill them. If she did, she would live in the shadows ever more.

Kill them? No. Revenge herself? No, at least not with blood.

Feeling a sudden relief, she pulled the fuse out of the cap, carefully put the dynamite back into a hollow in the rock nearby, took the fuse and tools and the cap away, and then returned, numbly, to her hideaway. She had just discovered her own boundaries. Maybe they were a woman's boundaries, this reluctance to take life or wreak revenge. Maybe it was more; a way of honoring Kermit.

She was blue. She was fighting to preserve the sole property remaining to her, fighting against a powerful, connected cabal of men without scruples, fighting to keep from being thrust into the streets, penniless. And now she faced the barrier of her own conscience, the inhibiting moral sense that would keep her from acting as recklessly as the cabal. No matter which way she turned, the other half of her rebelled. She berated herself for a lack of courage, of good Scots warrior instinct, but in the end, she knew that she could not take life. Some memory nagged her, some Scottish warrior woman back in the mists of time, some fierce and mythic woman who led the oppressed Scots against—something. She couldn't remember. But she did remember that the legendary woman—was her name Scáthach?—fought for her people, and not for her personal interests. For the Scots, not for herself. And not to keep a gold mine from being stolen by greedy and muscular crooks.

She settled in a blanket in her sanctuary, defeated, melancholic, and at war with herself. How could she stop this ruin of her property and life, if she couldn't muster the courage to fight back? Was it all because she was a woman, with a woman's respect for life? Was it because she possessed a womb, a way of making new life, a way of adding to the human race? She wished she could have been born without the inhibitions of conscience.

But she didn't sleep. Nothing was resolved. Tomorrow would only be worse than this day had been. There was no point even in occupying this hideaway if she wasn't going to fight for her mine by whatever means she could muster.

She awakened weary, under a clouded sky, with a chill breeze rolling down the mountains. She could not last here long, especially after the land froze, the berries vanished, and gradual starvation loomed. But as she began her day, she realized her restless night had carried her somewhere after all: toward goals. Her purpose was to possess her mine. And maybe sell it. Her purpose was to drive away the predators. Her task was to stop them cold. Each step they took toward stealing and looting her mine should have its consequences. Whatever they gained in law or by pillage, they should lose in some other way. And her purpose was to survive, feed, clothe, and shelter herself, and get on with life.

But how?

She didn't know. But it wouldn't ever happen if she continued on as an invisible wraith in the mountains around Helena. She could not be the lone wolf-woman haunting the peaks and hidden valleys, the outcast of the mountains. Her future lay in Marysville.

She collected her stuff, and stowed it far under the overhang, safe from weather, and safe from sight, unless someone happened squarely on the refuge. She washed carefully, and dressed herself as stylishly as she could, given her borrowed clothing. She had no looking glass to guide her, and no real comb, but she did have a ribbon to tie her chestnut hair together behind her head, which was the only grooming she could manage.

Then she set off, slipping through forest, down steep grades, as secretive as a deer, until she burst into the gulch and took its lonesome road into Marysville. She wondered whether she would ever see her mine again.

The town seemed strange to her; raucous in the morning, with wagons rattling on the clay road, shopkeepers sweeping their doorways, and off on the slope, the steady thump of the stamp mill, and the occasional rattle of tailings pouring out of ore cars onto an ever-expanding pile of waste rock. Noise and motion shattered the peace, unlike the soft sounds of her solitude on the mountain.

She headed straight for the constabulary and city hall, pulled open the heavy door, and discovered Constable Roach at his rolltop desk, penning some sort of material into a ledger.

"You, is it?" he asked, glancing at her, taking note of every detail. "This is the thirty-fourth day without an arrest, though I did permit one Jacob Morehouse to sleep off his indulgence in a cell with an unlocked door," he said. "We have a peaceful city without crime. Except now and then."

He reached into a cubbyhole in the desk and withdrew two thick folded papers, and handed them to her. "Another summons," he said. "Helena court. But no one knew how to deliver them to you, though of course every effort was made."

"You may tell me about them," she said. "It will save reading."

"They've expired. You were summoned to appear in District Court to answer a debt proceeding, the matter being what you owed the funeral home for services involving your late husband. Since then there's been a summary judgment; the mine was placed into public receivership, and sold to the highest bidder. And since there were none, the mine fell into the hands of Laidlow Funeral Home for the sum of the debt." He smiled. "That's all there is to it."

"And the debt has been discharged?"

"That's the second paper."

"How did the court know who owns the mine?"

"You didn't file any papers, that's how. It's all over with. The McPhee Mine is no longer in your hands, madam."

"It seems a little hasty; the mine's owners had not been notified."

"On the contrary, madam, advertisements were posted in the Helena and Marysville papers. And far be it for you to criticize our justice system. I don't think foreign-born people should object. Do you?"

"And what do you stand to gain from seizing the mine, Constable?"

The question caught him off guard. "Why do you ask such questions? Are you questioning the integrity of our judicial system?"

"Are you going to answer my question?"

"Well, it's none of your business, and that's my answer. Are we done?"

"No. Are you going to arrest me for vagrancy now?"

"I would imagine you'd best leave town as swiftly as possible, or face a night in that cell there, and forcible expulsion after paying a fine."

"And are you going to start mining the McPhee now?"

"Madam, we don't even know what's there. Laidlow was lucky to get the patent. Maybe it'll cover his debt, maybe not."

"He has the patent?"

"We will shortly; the original is missing."

"How could the court award the mine to anyone, then?"

"Madam, your confusions about law are not worth a response. You shouldn't worry your pretty head about things that require learning. Now you're wasting my time, and I'll expect you'll be out of town by sundown."

"You might as well put me in the cell right now," she said. "And you can go fetch a good meal from the eatery, and feed your prisoner. Because I'm not going anywhere. Jail food would taste just fine, don't you think?"

He rose, stiff in his thick blue uniform, brushed free of the last dog hair and dandruff, and loomed before her. He actually was a compact man, no larger than herself, but he was bristling, his trimmed beard was quivering, his forehead was furrowed.

"All the requirements of the law have been

answered," he said. "But I am quite capable of taking it into my own hands if duty requires it."

"What is your salary, Mr. Roach?"

"It's a matter of public record," he said, "but you're not public."

"You apparently aren't earning enough to satisfy your tastes."

He stared at her, unsure whether to take vast offense or dismiss her foolishness. Then he laughed. "I always enjoy a bold woman," he said.

He escorted her to the door, his hand forcibly steering her elbow, and then she was back in the bright, chill morning, with the sun struggling through whipping clouds. Well, she had learned something. Some sort of shabby proceedings had ripped the mine from her with rude haste, as if any delay might benefit her.

She stepped into the street, dodged some manure, and headed toward the office of her alleged lawyer, Hermes Apollo, who probably got his cut. But it would do no harm to find out.

SIXTEEN

Hermes Apollo greeted and dismissed her with a single glance.

"You've lost the mine. The Roach clan has it. Their pet judge handed it over." He eyed her. "That means I retract my proposal. I would marry a gold mine, but not a vagrant."

"Well, I would marry a lawyer, but not someone who thinks a bar exam is a look at a saloon."

He laughed. "But my offer of bed and board survives," he said.

"I'd be bored with your bed," she said.

He smiled blandly. "It's an offer you can't resist."

"They ran everything through the court in Helena, and hoped I wouldn't show up and fight," she said. "I just got these papers from Constable Roach."

"Oh, those. He didn't look very hard for you. That whole business, the funeral parlor lien, the alleged search for an owner, the seizure of the mine by the court, and the bidding on it—that was as good a joke as any. But maybe they didn't succeed. This came today."

He handed her an envelope from a federal government bureau. She extracted a parchment document marked FAIR COPY and notarized. It was Kermit's claim. But it was more. She was listed as one of the claimants. He had done that for her.

"All yours," he said. "If you can get it. The request for parish records in Scotland is not needed. You're named in the patent." He eyed her. "Now, do we marry, or do I bill you for services rendered?"

"I'll decide that whenever I feel like it," she said.

"My heart grows faint," he said.

"Where do I stand?"

"The mine? They have it. They'll exploit it. They'll occupy it and keep everyone else out. Especially you. If you take them to court, they'll delay the proceedings for years. By the time you have your day in court, after agreeing to pay me my high fees, of course, they'll have cleaned out the ore. A mine lasts only as long as there's ore, and usually not long."

"What do I do?"

"Find a husband. The town's full of suckers."

"You could buy me lunch."

"Actually, I was going to suggest that you buy me lunch. That might save me from billing you for services. And if you buy me lunch, it'll prove to me that you've set your cap for me."

She stared at his comfortable offices, with showy law books lining the walls, and massive oak furnishings.

"Good morning," she said.

He watched her leave. She doubted she would enter that office again. But at least she had something she didn't have before, a valid copy of the mine patent, and with her name on it, too. All she needed now was to take over the mine.

She stood in the street, near a fragrant pile of horse apples, unsure of what to do next. She was starved. She walked slowly toward Grand Street, and then to Mr. Wittgenstein's assay office.

The cowbells clanged when she entered the barren room.

He was back at the rear, loading one of his furnaces.

"In a minute," he said.

The room was very hot from escaped furnace heat. With tongs he slid several porcelain dishes into the fierce heat. Each dish had some sort of powder in it.

He closed the door of the furnace, and faced her. His forehead beaded with sweat.

"Expecting you," he said. "Do you still own the McPhee?"

"I do. I think."

"Some hooligans in here the other day, brought ore from your mine. I recognized it immediately. They wanted an assay. They also wondered if I was able to mill small quantities of ore. I said I was busy."

"Jerusalem Jones and Bum Carp. They're trying to clean out ore ahead of their relatives."

"I thought so. I did an assay anyway. That ore's getting better. If it continues, you've got a rich mine. But that's always a big if."

"I've been pushed out. Some fandango in the courts, and now the Roach people have it, and I can't get near it. But I have the patent. Right here. Would you like to buy the mine, Mr. Wittgenstein?"

It took a while to explain it all to him. She included Hermes Apollo's dark prediction that the mine would be exhausted before she could take it back, even assuming she could find a lawyer able and willing to pursue a years-long struggle, all for a percent of an unproven mine.

He sighed, stared out the small window, and shook his head. "The deck's stacked," he said. "I can't afford lawyers for several years, with no certainty about what might result. Not even a group of investors could."

"Thought I'd ask," she said.

He was staring bleakly. "Mrs. McPhee, there's one thing I can do. I can let you know what is happening inside the mine. Assayers know that."

She smiled and nodded.

There were walls in Marysville, invisible ones, higher than she could climb. She stood in the street, wondering what next. Then, almost involuntarily, she made her way to the Laidlow Funeral Home, entered, and found Mortimer Laidlow himself.

"Well, if it isn't Mrs. McPhee," he said,

appearing almost magically from behind red velvet drapes. She noted his rum-soaked nose, its capillaries blooming. And his pocked cheeks, probably from a losing bout with adolescence.

"You want another body?" she asked.

"We're always ready to help the bereaved," he said in a practiced manner.

"I could come up with one. Who would you prefer to embalm?"

"We never jest about these sacred things, madam."

"You might try it on your lackeys here, Mr. Jones and Mr. Carp. I do believe they've been gouging quartz out of my mine without your knowledge or consent. Some of it's stored at the assay office. They would both look handsome in a casket, the best that money can buy."

It took a moment to process that, during which his cheek twitched and his fingers diddled.

"They were hard at work, last I knew. Stealing can inspire some serious labor, if the theft seems profitable enough."

"Ah, I trust I misheard you. You referred to your mine?"

"I did."

"I'm afraid you've been away too long, madam. The courts have found for me."

"I know all about the courts, and their jack-rabbit justice, and I'll tell you it's my mine, and I own the patent, and here it is."

She held it before the man, careful not to let him snatch it away. "I was the co-owner of the patent, and as the survivor, the sole owner. This is a fair copy, notarized with the embossed seal of the bureau."

She snatched it away before he could put his mitts on it.

His oleaginous smile, funereal in all its glory, twitched through his face. He sighed. "It's too late, my dear lady. The courts have transferred unclaimed property to me, because I held a lien against it. You'd best just consider that paper a bit of history."

"It's a gold mine, my gold mine."

"Ah, yes, sometimes the bereaved delude themselves, thinking their loved one lives on, a spark that will burst into renewed life, even during the last rites."

"You're a corker, you are."

She had expected as much. "Mr. Laidlow, bring me a sheet of paper, an ink bottle, a blotter, and a nib pen."

He smiled. "Your last will and testament. I have these things right here, at my desk."

He led her to a small, discreet desk, the place where rites and services and payment were usually negotiated, and he produced a sheet of good white vellum.

She dipped the pen, dated the sheet, and began:

"Herewith is notice that you are to vacate the

McPhee Mine within twenty-four hours of the above date, and to cease removing ore from it. Failure to do so will result in whatever action the owner deems necessary to prevent theft and trespassing."

She put her name to it and handed it to him.

He read it, making a great effort to look amused.

"I will share it with the other owners," he said. "It's the property of the Roach Group, you know. A trust company."

"You've been served," she said. "And do share it with the rest. That makes more witnesses. Especially, share it with Constable Roach. I don't know his given name, but it doesn't matter. I'll find out."

"The bereaved have strange ideas," he said. "Sometimes it is necessary to commit them to Warm Springs. The Territory's asylum for unfortunates," he said. He was acting twitchy.

"Is that a threat?"

"We do what we can for unfortunates."

She rose quietly, smiled at him, which evoked another twitch, and headed for fresh air. Why did nature seem so clean, and interiors in Marysville seem so unclean?

She stood in the sun a moment, feeling her stomach hurt, and noted that it was nearly noon. Maybe Tip Leary would be on hand. She found the double doors unlocked, and entered, smacking into the stale ale smell of the place that she remembered. And he was there, sitting at the end of the battered bar, keeping his ledgers.

"You, is it? Some sunshine in Tip's grog shop?"

"You mind if I dig into your pretzels, Tip?"

He eyed her closely, saw she was in need, and handed her the jar. And the other one with the pickled eggs.

"Seems to me I'd better close this place for a little bit, to keep it legal," he said, and ambled to his doors and shut them. "The law says ladies and saloons are mutually exclusive."

She tackled a big, salty pretzel, and another, and started on a third before she was ready to talk, which he watched closely.

He found some sarsaparilla, and poured it for her, and she sipped it gratefully.

"Now, then," she said, and plunged in. She had to go back a ways, to her life day after day in a hideaway of her own fashioning. The patent with her name on it. Roach's court papers that he had neglected to serve in a timely way. And the arrival of the Laidlow hooligans, and the rest, up to her visit with the mortician himself. Then, suddenly, she was worn out.

"And you haven't a roof over your head, or more than what you wear."

"I have my hideaway. I can live there a while more, before they find me out."

"You're a bird with a broken nest, and the chicks all gone," he said.

"I'd like a safe place. Now, with this patent, proof of my ownership, I'm ready to do what I can."

Tip shook his head. "When the courts aren't good and true, and when they're robbing your mine while keeping you out, and while the lawyers land low punches and charge you high, while all that's going on, you're without a nest, without a meal—but not without friends."

He eyed the small wind-up clock at the end of the back bar, and made a decision.

"Rest a little at your hideaway, where you'll be safe. Then make your way here about midnight, and there'll be hands to guide you to a safe place, and other hands to put a little food in you, and other hands to watch over you through the days to come."

"Tip, what are you saying?"

"I'm saying a widow has friends in my saloon, and these friends, they'll find a nest for ye, and keep you fed, and give you a safe place here in town, and whatever you do up at the mine, ye have a place that's tight and silent."

"They'd do that?"

"They'd do more than that. They tried to drill and muck for you, but got chased away. They were ready to dig ore, get your little debt paid down. Count on it. Come by when the saloons shut down. There'll be a lamp in my window here to let you know, and I'll be here to introduce you to some lads who'll look after you."

162

She stood, refreshed by the small meal, drew him to her, kissed him, and headed into the bright day.

"Take a couple of pretzels with you," he said.

SEVENTEEN

March didn't know whether it was midnight. She only knew the night was long when she started down the obscure forest trails in deep dark.

She had toiled her way back to her hideaway, rested, and gathered what little clothing she possessed in a burlap sack, and then decided to peek at the McPhee Mine. She had worked her way through densely forested slopes to a place where she could observe, and what she saw stirred bitterness.

A crew of maybe a dozen men had been prepping the mine. Some were adding trestle that would take the ore cars to a good waste dump site. Timber men were cutting posts and crossbeams, putting in the shoring that Kermit could never afford. Other men were erecting a storage shed outside of the mine head.

She had watched darkly, and then retreated to her hideaway. She knew it wouldn't stay a hideout for long; those men would fan out, hunting for new deposits nearby, and they would happen upon the little refuge under the overhang. She was escaping to Marysville just in time.

Now, with a thin moon to help her, she eased through deep night, stumbling over deadfall, until at last she reached Long Gulch and the trail into Marysville. Then the walk was easy. The trail led not only to the McPhee, but other outlying mines in the area, and was well used. The Drumlummon was the primary mine in the district, but now there were several more, which was one reason Marysville prospered.

The town lay quiet, the miners' cabins dark, the lamps in the saloons turned down. Nothing prowled but cats, which were prized in mining towns because they killed rats, which were the unseen plague of most mining districts.

One lamp burned softly at Tipperary Leary's saloon, the light welcoming and gentle. She found the door unlocked, and found Tip dozing, along with two miners she didn't know.

"Good," Tip said. "These two, they've stayed up to be looking after you. They'll take you to your fancy new home."

"But Tip, I don't need . . ."

"Be quiet, will ye? Here's the thing. There's about twenty of my patrons in the know. You'll have food daily. Not fancies, but things to keep you fed. It takes a bit out of their brown envelope to do it, but every one's pledged to it, for as long as you need a little something to fill the stomach. Now, you'll be staying on an estate. Not Tommy Cruse's own digs, but the washerwoman house in the back. Cruse got rich, built this place, sold the Drumlummon to a big corporation, moved himself and his brood to Helena, but hung on to the house. He's got a little sentiment about Marysville, having started it and named it and saw it grow to three thousand. This washerwoman cottage, it's back in a grove of aspen so thick it's not seen from the house. There's a room for the woman, and a room to wash, with a stove and big tubs and drying lines outside. The Cruses, they ran through sheets and tablecloths and their own clothing enough to keep a hired woman busy. But they're gone, and she's gone, and the place lies in a grove of trees that will keep it from prying eyes."

"Oh, Tip."

"These two are Monk and Brian, and they'll take you now." He reached for a jar. "And have a pretzel."

They took her into the night. Marysville slept. But the stamp mill on the slope still thundered, muted violence reducing rock to powder. It was like a heartbeat. She followed them through the chill. The town lay near the continental divide, and was rarely warm. They steered her into an open field with a large white home in the middle of it, every window black and lonely.

"That's the Cruse house, ma'am. They find Helena more to their taste now, since he pocketed a million and more," Monk said.

"That's the washhouse yonder," Brian said. "We've fixed it up a little."

They led her into an obscure building. She could

166

see nothing until Brian lit a candle. It was snug and bare, the cot without bedclothes, the room naked. But it looked like paradise to her.

Brian deposited some things atop a cold stove. "This'll keep you. It's just oats and potatoes, but there's a little split wood there, and all the fixings, and you can boil up what you need. The aspens, they'll hide the smoke."

"May I ask why—all this?"

"You were born with a four-leaf clover in your hand," Monk said.

She wouldn't let go of it. "There's more to it, I think."

"What Tipperary Leary says, that's how it goes," Monk said.

"There is more, I think."

Brian grinned. "Sure is, ma'am, but we'll let it go just the way it is."

"Is it the constable?"

"There's food here for a few days, and we'll be checking. And if it's not enough, give Tip the word."

"How may I thank you?"

"We've got to get some shut-eye, ma'am. Shift comes soon."

Brian blew out the candle, and they were suddenly gone, in a rush of night air. Except for the distant thump of the mill, it was suddenly quiet. She was pierced by loneliness. Not just for her benefactors, but for her husband and son, not to mention all her family across the sea. Give her a nest, and she ached to fill it.

She felt oddly comfortable, as if destined to be led to this place. There was some settling in to do, but she put it off, wrapped her blanket about her, and found comfort and peace on the cot. The odd thing of it was her sense of coming home. She had taken possession, even though she had yet to explore the building or the washroom, or the glade of aspen that hid it from the Cruse house.

Just at dawn a train whistle awakened her, and she remembered that Marysville was connected by a Northern Pacific spur to Helena, and that the railroad brought mining timbers, coal, food, and necessaries to this mountain-girt town. She arose swiftly, eager to explore this barren cottage. She stepped into the laundry room, jacked a pump, and was rewarded with cold water. She stepped outside, and found herself in a glade of trees, with windows opening on the blue mountains. She could see the road up Long Gulch that would take her to the McPhee Mine and her hideaway. To go back and forth she wouldn't even need to go through Marysville, so long as there was no fence—and she saw none.

The cottage cookstove was tiny and efficient, and with just a few sticks of kindling she had water boiling for some porridge. It all seemed a miracle to her, and gave rise to the idea that maybe, with this heartening refuge, she could survive here. Maybe she could become a washer-woman. Everything she needed to make a living was right there. But she would need the owner's permission. She did not scorn ordinary labor. That had been her lot as a mother and wife, and always would be. She might even be the town washerwoman, if need be.

But first, the mine. There had to be a way. She did not know Constable Roach's hours, but she suspected he was more or less on duty all the time, sometimes in his office, sometimes patrolling the bustling town, sometimes making appearances in saloons after dark. She would begin with the constable, and maybe she could learn a few things. Or maybe she could give him the same ultimatum she had given to his brother-in-law, Mortimer Laidlow.

When the day was bright and quick, she headed into Marysville, found the constabulary, and found him making entries in a ledger.

"You again, is it?" he asked, studying her clean dress and well-washed face.

"I've some questions, Constable. If you have time."

"I don't. And you're wasting what little I have."

"You could begin by telling me who or what claims to own the McPhee Mine. I wish to know."

"You needn't bother your head about it. It's a corporation."

"And who might that be?"

He sighed, annoyed, and flecked a bit of lint off his immaculate blue uniform. "It happens to be a family business. My family. The Roaches, Laidlows and in-laws, and certain cousins, about a dozen of us in all. We've business interests in Marysville. We own the restaurant that feeds my prisoners, we own the city water company. We own the coal, ice, and firewood dealership. We own a grocery. We own a blacksmith, a bakery, and a livery barn. And we now have an interest in five of the twenty mines in the district."

"And your cousin is a district judge."

He suddenly retreated into himself.

"The judge helped your company acquire properties?"

"He is not a principal. Entirely independent, of course. Now, madam, you've been asked to leave Marysville, and you are defying me. You are a vagrant. And it seems a public nuisance. What shall I do? Tell me."

"Restore my mine to me. As you should. As conscience requires."

He laughed, a dry, rheumy cackle. "You are a one-woman variety show," he said.

"Mind if I use a sheet of paper and your pen?"

He smiled thinly, and nodded.

She collected pen, ink bottle, blotter, and paper, and wrote a notice, similar to the one she had given Laidlow, directing the Roach interests to abandon her property, cease trespassing, cease stealing ore, and to remove themselves within twenty-four hours. This time she signed it and added another line. "Owner of the patent of the McPhee Mine."

She blotted it and handed it to the constable, who read it with delight wreathing his carefully groomed features.

"You know," he said, "I was talking to my brother-in-law, and we both thought that Marysville is suffering from the presence of a most afflicted woman, plainly alone, without means, and brimming with dementia. She needs supervision. She seems to live on what she can pluck out of trash piles. Fortunately, the Territory has a fine new asylum at Warm Springs for the mad. It seems to me that I would be doing a service to you, as well as my city, to petition the court to commit you. You could spend the rest of your life protected from yourself, safe, comfortable, and no menace to the community."

He plainly was enjoying himself.

"See that cell?" she said. "You're on the wrong side of the bars."

She left, steaming. But maybe she had achieved something. She'd given notice. And by giving notice, she could justify whatever she would be forced to do.

She headed next for the Drumlummon Mill, the noisy monster that rumbled on a slope, processing tons of gold ore daily. These were male precincts, and she scarcely knew where to turn. Smoke billowed from stacks. Rank odors rode the breezes. Working men were moving material in and out of giant doors. From within she heard the clatter of metal on metal, and smelled the acrid smoke of fierce furnaces.

She was looking for a building or office that might house a manager, but the structures were all raw wood, grayed by weather, not even coated with whitewash. No one in this place was spending a spare nickel on any amenity. She kept working upslope, finding nothing resembling an office, and finally worked down to the base, and there she did find a long gray structure, plain as a warehouse, and an unmarked door that seemed the likely place. She entered. It was indeed an office, a big bullpen with some clerks, and a private office to the left.

The clerks were startled by a female presence, but in due course they steered her to the office of the manager, a muttonchopped man named Burroughs.

"Madam?" he asked, plainly wanting to get it over with.

"I am March McPhee. I own the McPhee Mine. I have the patent right here."

She brandished it. He read it swiftly.

"My mine has been commandeered. It was taken, not sold, after my husband died. I've demanded that the occupants leave at once and cease mining. Now, sir, I am requiring you not to mill any McPhee ore, and to pay me for whatever gold or other minerals have been extracted from my ore at the mill. And pay me from the beginning. From the first load they brought you for custom milling."

The man's muttonchops seemed to ripple as he shifted chewing tobacco about in his cavernous mouth.

"You have proof of ownership, I suppose?" he asked.

"I have just shown it to you. And if you continue to refine my ore without paying me, or shipping the ore to me, you will find yourself in court."

"They own it now, I'm sure."

"Ask them for a bill of sale signed by me. Ask to see their ownership papers."

He smiled at last. "There's nothing I can do, madam," he said. "Nothing at all."

EIGHTEEN

Stubborn, that's what she was. She needed to talk to the district judge in Helena, Samuel Roach was his name, and set the record straight. Maybe it would do no good. But she had her patent, and she could tell him about the summons that his cousin, the constable, failed to deliver to her in a timely way, and see what that would do.

The trouble was, she hadn't a dime to go there. Helena, the county seat as well as the new Territorial capital, lay about thirty miles distant, on a hogleg route. A Northern Pacific spur served the mining town. It plugged into the mainline near Helena.

There must be a way.

The next day she visited the tiny station; it stood near the Drumlummon Mine. The station master was present only an hour before the daily run. She entered the depot, studied the wicket of the master, found the time of the arrival and departure chalked on a blackboard, and also noted a price. A dollar and twenty cents round-trip; seventy-five cents one way. There wasn't a soul in the little structure.

But on a gravel platform outside, she discovered an old man on a bench, soaking up summer sun.

"One train a day? For passengers?" she asked him.

He eyed her with watery blue eyes, from behind a scraggly beard. "If that," he said. "Mixed lot; one old coach behind a string of boxcars or gondolas. You go to Helena, you stay over for the night, or walk home."

"What's in the freight cars, sir?"

"Heavy equipment, mining stuff, coming in; certain ores that can better be reduced at the smelter east of Helena, going out. A few carloads of foodstuffs, hardware, mercantile whatnots. Once in a while, a stock car, usually with hogs. We got enough ranchers around to run beef in."

"Hogs?"

"Yep, Marysville miners eat hogs like we was born to it. A hog car announces itself on the wind, if it's blowing toward town."

"And the hog cars go back empty?"

"You can't put anything into a hog car. They don't smell like a good Smithfield Ham, I'll tell you." He eyed her. "You're mighty curious about it."

"I don't have the price of a ticket," she said.

The geezer broke into a gap-toothed smile. "Just find yourself a boxcar and enjoy the ride. And don't wear skirts. They'll likely get caught and pull you under."

"Who checks the cars?"

"Anyone. Brakeman, railroad dicks, who knows?

You'd not be the first to slick it over on the old Northern Pacific."

"How do I get on, with the station right here?"

"Opposite side, and make sure no fireman or engineer's looking back."

"And if I hop a freight coming back here, is it the same thing in Helena?"

"Play it by ear, old gal. It's one long walk from there to here. Take it from an old bindlestiff."

"What's that?"

"Tramp, lady. You're talking to a retired tramp."

She studied the layout. The tracks dead-ended at the mine, not far away. There was not a single structure or tree that might conceal her if she were to hop the freight. The whole idea was daunting. Not only hop the freight here, but also in Helena. And make sure it was the Marysville local, and not some mainline train. And know when it left. And dodge the railroad dicks.

The old codger spat, a fine brown stream of well-used tobacco, and wiped his dirty beard.

"Here's what you do," he said. "You dress fancy, maybe add a hat, and climb right up the steps and into the caboose. The coach's up front, right behind the engine. Stubby little six-wheeler. Then there's a string of freight, and the caboose. There'll be a brakeman around there, maybe right at the steps. You just say something like, 'You taking me to Helena?' Like that. He will or he won't. Pretty lady like you, he just might."

She phrased it delicately. "And will I owe him anything? An obligation?"

"Beats me," he said. "Never knew much about women."

That didn't exactly answer her question. His gap-toothed grin didn't either.

"The next train out leave in the morning? At seven?"

"Before I'm up and stirring," he said. "Stay clear of the station."

She resolved to be on it. Scots were thrifty.

But she'd still have to find the courthouse, hope court wasn't in session, locate his chamber, and try to talk her way in. And whatever the result, figure out how to get back into the mountains again.

She spent that day assembling something to eat on her trip. She scarcely knew how, given how little she had, but eventually baked some oatmeal cakes, and those would have to do. But she lacked a handbag; nothing in that barren washerwoman house helped her. Well then, she would go hungry.

Early the next morning she garbed herself in borrowed skirts, not a bit satisfied with any of it, and headed for the little station. A dozen people stood patiently on the gravel platform, so she stood well away, the sightseer. She knew she was conspicuous but there was no help for it. In time, a stubby engine chuffed in, raining cinders and belching smoke from a diamond stack. There was a battered wine-colored coach, three boxcars, two gondolas filled with some sort of ore, and a gray caboose. The train shielded her from the station, so she stepped across the creosoted tracks, fragrant in the morning sun, and eased toward the caboose. There was a small stair at the rear, with handrails, and she would have to step high to board.

She didn't hesitate. But the moment she stepped up, a brakeman in blue yelled.

"Hey! Off of there."

The young man materialized from somewhere forward, maybe between the caboose and the last gondola.

"What do you think you're doing?"

"I'm Scots," she said.

He stared. "Scots is it? That answers it. I do not see you."

"And yourself?"

"Half Swede, half bobcat," he said.

She stepped in, fascinated by the compact comfort she found there, including a small table, benches, potbellied stove with a cooktop, and even a bunk. But most of the space was given to equipment, especially lamps, flares, and tools. The open window was letting in soot, even while the train was boarding passengers up ahead. She settled in a seat, heard some shouts and clanging, a whistle, a jolt as the couplings pulled tight, and then the caboose rolled slowly forward, even as the brakeman swung onboard.

He sat down, stared a moment, and settled the matter in his mind. "I don't see you. When we reach the Helena yards, I will step down ahead of you, and yell when it's okay."

"Scots are invisible," she said.

"I suppose it's none of my business," he said.

"I'm going to ask a judge to give me my gold mine back."

He plainly didn't know how to respond to that. "I earn a dollar fifty a day," he muttered.

"That's a dollar fifty more than I do."

"Good luck," he said.

"Don't wish you could trade positions or fates with me," she said. "My mine was stolen."

"I could use a gold mine."

The train wove downslope on shoddy roadbed, never getting up speed as slopes rose and fell, and forests crowded the right of way. She wondered why a spark hadn't ignited the thick-clad alpine slopes any hot summer. It was glorious country, still somehow virgin even if miners were burrowing into every likely outcrop.

They reached a relatively flat area, and then switched onto the NP mainline, whose silvery rails stretched straight into the Territorial capital.

"Do you know where the county courthouse is?" she asked.

"Yeah, they fined me there once, five clams for getting into a fight. It's on Broadway."

"Wherever that is," she said.

Helena was a mongrel place, half gold-mining camp, half emerging capital of Montana. Last Chance Gulch had yielded a torrent of placer gold, and the city's commercial buildings had risen right beside the twisting bonanza gulch. Its natural beauty had drawn the newly rich, and these people had built stately brick homes on one side of the gulch, while the less fortunate crowded helterskelter into chaotic neighborhoods on the other. All the other mining districts in the area, including Marysville, were satellites of the fabulous Last Chance Gulch, where placer gold was discovered by four Georgians fleeing the Civil War.

The brakeman proved to be a lively conspirator, and at the right moment he summoned March from the caboose, nodded, and headed up the line of cars. She studied the sidings, saw nothing to stop her, and stepped delicately across steel rails, to a platform mostly empty, and then headed into the city, which was a long walk away. She was hungry, but that couldn't be helped.

Helena struck her as a city divided. Workingmen in dungarees toiled everywhere, but along the streets she discovered clerical sorts, men in suits and cravats and bowlers, some with elaborate mustachios or muttonchops, the hirsute gentlemen of Helena plainly the upper class.

Somehow, Helena was different. Here people wrestled for power and fame; she could see it in the mansions rising on one side of town. It didn't seem friendly, the way Marysville did. But what did it matter? She found Broadway, turned there where the street climbed away from the gulch, passed the redbrick federal assay office, and found the Lewis and Clark County Courthouse easily enough. She marveled. The city had existed only a few years, but here was a substantial stone building surrounded by landscaped lawn. Gold had profited the county.

It was late in the morning. She entered the building, walked on waxed hardwood floors, her steps echoing in the high hall, found the courtroom, which was empty, and found the chambers. She was in luck. She entered, and the door closed behind her with a soft snap. A clerk in shirtsleeves, with a garter on one arm, eyed her.

"I wish to see Judge Roach," she said.

"He's busy. But you could try tomorrow. He's got a session this afternoon."

"Tell him it's March McPhee, and I own the McPhee Mine, and I've come from Marysville."

"I tell you, he's busy and won't see anyone."

"Tell him."

Something in her tone must have changed his mind. He eyed her, rose reluctantly, and vanished into the chambers, separated from the anteroom by a pebbled glass door.

She didn't know what she would say. She would show him the patent, and show him the summons that were never delivered. And ask for a reconsideration.

The clerk returned. "Be brief," he said.

March McPhee entered, found that the judge bore a family resemblance to the constable, but had full black beard and agate eyes.

"It is unlawful to attempt to influence or bribe a judge," he said, in a voice so quiet that March strained to hear it. "Watch what you say, and if you transgress, I'll call the bailiff."

"Thank you for the warm welcome," she said.

His coal eyes bore into her.

"Here is a fair copy of the patent on the McPhee Mine, listing me as one of the owners. Here are two court papers that Constable Roach carefully neglected to give me in time, leaving me in the dark about what happened here."

"And what happened here, madam?"

"A sham proceedings that took my mine from me."

"What makes you think that?"

"Because the whole event was staged to steal my mine from me after my husband died."

"Contempt of court," he said. "I'll summon the bailiff, and you may cool your heels in my hospitality parlor and stay there for as long as I deem you in contempt. Which may be some little while."

He rang a bell, and a burly bailiff swiftly arrived.

"Lock her up," the judge said.

The bailiff grinned.

March McPhee refused to march, and the bailiff had to drag her away.

NINETEEN

The cell was small, cold, and dark. Iron bars pinned her in. A small window high up let in sunlight, hope, and dreams of liberty. A sheet-iron platform served as a bunk and seat. An open bucket served as a chamber pot. The iron-barred door clanged shut behind her, and the bailiff turned away. The silence that followed was the quietness of a tomb. Jail was all about silence; being taken away from busy commerce and human voice.

She surveyed this dour and odorous place with a great sadness. She was helpless now. Her fate rested entirely with the judge. She knew that contempt of court meant that the judge could keep her there as long as he chose, without trial, bail, recourse. He could do with her as he would, for she was no more than a rag doll now.

She peered out, onto a bleak corridor, painted brown, seeing and hearing nothing. She appeared to be the sole prisoner in the county lockup. There would be no one next door, or down the corridor, to talk to, share misery with.

She paced the cell, three steps in any direction, and felt it close down upon her. She ached suddenly for exercise. Walking seemed like the ultimate comfort, or even luxury. Walking to somewhere.

She swiftly realized the dilemma. Time. How could she fill it? What could she do? Were there exercises of the mind she might pursue? She saw not a thing to read. There was no one to talk to. The tick of an imaginary clock sliced her life away, minute by minute.

Finally she lay down on the hard bench, its boards cruel against her flesh. This would be her bed, her sole comfort, for as long as Judge Roach chose to keep her penned. She thought of her Kermit, and of her lost baby, but that only deepened her sadness. She thought of Scotland, her parents' cottage, her girlhood, her mother, and that worsened the ache within her. Finally she drifted into a passive state of emptiness, and let the hours tick by.

When the light in the window darkened, a warden came at last, bearing a bowl of gruel and a spoon. She eyed him, an elderly big-bellied man, probably a political appointee.

But at least he was cheery. "Brought you some chowder, courtesy of Lewis and Clark County. I guess you riled up the judge, eh?"

"I asked for a proper hearing."

He laughed, and she suspected he had heard it all before. He handed her the bowl through an iron service door. The slop was cold. She lifted it, took the spoon, tasted it, and then threw it all in his face.

He laughed. "That's what he said, crazy as a

loon," he said. "Guess you'll start to lose a few pounds. Oh, that will add a little to your time here."

He wandered off, and she wondered what had gotten into her. She had always prided herself on her serenity and self-control. It had all exploded like a fulminate of mercury cap, snap, over before she'd warned herself against foolishness.

It was worse than that. The old man hadn't said one word that could be considered offensive. A cynical laugh, perhaps, but not anything that justified a bowl of stew on his head.

She was hungry, but the remains of the meal lay sprayed across a filthy cement floor, mixed with whatever body fluids were embedded there. The silence returned, and she slipped to the bench and let its hard surface offend her soft body.

A deep sense of helplessness becomes, in the end, an ally, and now she lay through a black night on her iron bed, the absence of hope easing the hours away. Once she made use of the terrible bucket, and then swiftly slid into an estate somewhere between wakefulness and stupor.

Dawn came, quietness without food or drink, and her body was telling her about it. But lying quietly was better than pacing the cage, or yelling for help that would not come.

She lay back, unable to better her condition, and then she did hear a clang, and the pad of footsteps, and found herself staring through bars at the judge. He wore a black suit. For a moment they simply gazed, she upward, and he downward.

"I have some papers for you to sign," he said.

"And then what?"

"I'll decide after you sign them."

She sat up, brushed her soiled skirts, and waited.

"There's a small problem. I hear you like to throw things. Like this ink bottle in my hand. Or this pen. That would be most unfortunate. So the best I can manage is to hand you the pen, fresh from the bottle, which will remain in my hand, and you can put your John Henry, or maybe I should call it your Joan of Arc, on these."

"What are they?" she asked.

"One is a transfer of title of the McPhee federal patent to the Roach Group. The other is a bill of sale of the mine to the Roach Group, for services rendered, including debt repayment."

He smiled benignly.

"I will read them," she said.

"Nice facility we have here," he said. "We're the first county in the Territory to have a courthouse with a modern, comfortable jail."

She stood, and he handed the two documents to her.

"When the pen needs a dip in the inkwell, hand it to me," he said, and handed her the nib pen.

She studied the documents, which were full of boilerplate and had false dates, stemming back to the court proceedings she had missed.

"What does this get me?" she asked.

"Sign and get it over with. I'm a busy man," he said.

"I'm stubborn," she said, and slowly ripped the two documents in shreds, and tucked the pieces in her bosom where she thought they would be safe.

He reddened, bloated, shrank, and smiled.

"They were right," he said. "Mad as a hatter. Very well, then. Enjoy your stay."

She threw the pen at him, but it hit a bar and fell.

She heard his footsteps retreat down the dark corridor, a clang, and then the oppressive silence settled over her again, but now she was thirsty as well as hungry. She wondered what had gotten into her this time. She could have signed and walked out. Maybe. She thought there may have been a few aces up his sleeve, little unpleasantries awaiting her after she had signed away her mine and veneered his clan's theft with the look of pure innocence.

She settled back upon her bed of thorns, for there was nothing else to do, and waited, because there was nothing else to think of.

The wait wasn't long. A pear-shaped man appeared and eyed her kindly.

"So you're the one," he said. "Have an apple."

He held a beautiful red apple in his hand, and she swiftly took it. The apple was gloriously sweet and moist, and she wolfed two or three bites while he watched. Only then did she study her visitor, who was now sitting comfortably on a stool on the other side of the gray iron bars. He wore a brown tweed suit, a red cravat, and lace-up shoes in need of polish. His round face was made all the broader by thick muttonchops. But he had merry brown eyes under thick lids and rolls of flesh below.

"Smells here," he said. "No one wants to be in a prison for long. And that's what bothers me. You seem to want to."

"Who did you say you are?"

"I didn't. I practice allopathic medicine. You know, the sort that is not homeopathic."

She was too busy devouring the apple to care.

"Yes, allopathic's the wave of the future. It enlists science," he said. "It enrolls pragmatism. It bases itself on hypothesis, experimentation, and verification. Unlike any other sort."

She ate the core of the apple, seeds and all, everything but the stem.

"We always diagnose with caution because there's so much we don't know. But it pays off. We're more likely to be right, and helpful to our patients, than any other branch." He studied her. "Now then. You look a little worse for wear, and I wonder why you don't simply walk out. You've had a chance."

"Because I believe in justice."

"That sounds a little like paranoia, wouldn't you say?"

She fell into silence, suddenly seeing which way this was going.

"Here you are, stuck in a terrible place, and free to walk away just by signing a bill of sale, I take it. But instead, you are seeing phantasms and demons. Have you always been this way?"

"What way?"

He shrugged. "You tell me."

"What did you say your name is?"

He shook his head. "I didn't say. You must be imagining things. A head full of phantasms."

"What is your name?"

"J. Bark Laidlow. The J stands for Jerrold. My MD derives from Curtis Correspondence College, in Peoria."

"You too," she said.

He smiled. "Oh, yes, I'm the younger brother of Mort. The family joke is, he plants my mistakes."

"And why are you here?"

"To evaluate you for Warm Springs. The Territory does take kind care of those who are non compos mentis."

"And am I?"

"Well, I have it from my cousin that you not only refused to sign a perfectly ordinary sales agreement, but that you collected each and every piece and stuffed it in your, ah, bosom. Now tell me, why did you do that? Worthless paper? Scraps of refuse?"

"Because it might be valuable."

"Now you do arouse my curiosity."

She hesitated, and then rushed ahead. "It's evidence. Fraudulent dates on both."

He laughed. "Oh, my, you are a bit off-kilter. What do you think we should do about it?"

"Return my mine patent, which the judge has, set me free, and put me out on the streets."

"I'm afraid that's pure fantasy, and has nothing to do with reality, Mrs. McPhee. Here you are, in contempt of court, no sign of rational thought, no proposal to remedy your contempt by signing the documents, no sign that you really grasp the grave nature of your dementia, or are living in a real world." He sighed. "No, it's clear from this extensive evaluation that it would be better for the Territory if you were to spend time in our facility. There are a variety of treatments intended to restore you to your senses, ranging from electromagnetic shocks to therapeutic enemas."

"If that's the price of signing, you'll learn I'm stubborn."

"Rigid is the word, madam. Rigidity is a mark of the deranged soul. A healthy mind bends, flexes, adapts. But one who is so set upon a course that she can't change, well, there's deep, deep trouble afoot. And I should add that you become a menace to society. What if in your sad condition you should decide to violate the laws of man and God, and do something very dark? We can't have that. What if voices drive you to commit mayhem? You would be powerless to resist, and you might imperil the lives of countless worthy citizens."

She saw how this was going, and oddly didn't mind, if it got her out of this dark hellhole.

He paused. "Well, you can still prove your serene good health to me if you wish."

She shook her head.

"It's a simple matter. I have, here, copies of the papers you are now harboring in your sweet bosom, and I have also pen and blotter and ink. First, you will need to extract those sad shards of paper you in your delusions scooped up, and give them to me. Second, you will sign both papers and I will witness. Third, I will send Judge Roach word that you are sober, sane, and repentant. And I expect he will send word to set you free, providing you take the next train out."

He pulled the papers out of a portfolio, along with the writing instruments.

"Bring in some fresh air," she said. "The place is all stunk up."

He shook his head in resignation. "My findings are most dismaying," he said. "It is needful to commit you to Warm Springs. Dementia praecox."

192

TWENTY

The beauty of Warm Springs surprised March. The asylum sat in a broad, bright valley rimmed by mountains. A warm spring nearby burbled from a limestone cone. The Territorial asylum, begun in 1877 even as the Sioux war raged in the eastern half of the Territory, was a generous structure with dormitories for men and women, and one for dangerous inmates, along with service and dining facilities. The windows opened on noble panoramas, and the dormitories were bright and airy, fresh and clean. There were extensive gardens, worked by those who were suited, which grew much of the food for the inmates.

But the rooms were populated by odd, tragic, and sad mortals, deemed mad, even as the court had deemed her mad, a stain that would be upon her the rest of her days. A sheriff's deputy was assigned to bring her there. She wasn't shackled, but nonetheless a captive, as any criminal in transit might be. Trains carried them to Butte, and then Anaconda, and horse and carriage brought them to Warm Springs, where the bored deputy delivered his charge and vanished.

The matron of the women's ward, Mrs. Botts, took over, showed March her bunk, asked about any special health needs, and warned March to be obedient, behave, or she could be deprived of her "privileges," whatever those were. The woman was big, tough, had red work-coarsened hands that looked capable of beating someone to pulp, so March listened warily, paid heed to the rules, which were not numerous, and kept her counsel. There were twenty-three other females enclosed with her, kept in the hall by a locked door. She eyed them. Some stared vacantly at the ceiling. One or two groaned and sobbed incessantly. One sat in a chair slapping herself, as if under siege from a thousand gnats or spiders. One was a midget with forlorn eyes, who seemed to be imprisoned only because of her odd nature.

Some looked ready to befriend March, and she knew she would find out which ones could be actual friends, and which ones would only spout gibberish. But for the moment, she studied the surrounding landscape. The Clark Fork River cut through the Deer Lodge valley, on its way to the western sea. This was the Columbia River drainage. Even as she studied that broad and open land, she was dreaming of escape. This could not be the end of her life. This could not be where she would exist, alone and forgotten, until she grew weak and faded away.

She knew that this lightly guarded place would offer its chance in due course, but she would have to make good on it or be put in the guarded ward for dangerous and demented mortals. And she knew at once that the difficulty would not be in walking away, but getting away, through open fields with no camouflage, no place to hide, no way to disappear. Indeed, the very clothing they gave her would mark her in the event she sought help. Food, water, shelter, a map, a compass, a plan, a refuge. But she was March McPhee, and she would do whatever she could, and if she failed she'd do it again, and again, and again, because that was the only way she could regain her life.

Was it all for gold? Had that cabal of relatives killed her baby, robbed her, stolen her mine, railroaded her here, for gold? Violated every decency for gold? Rolled over a newly widowed woman for gold? Condemned her to the life of a reputed madwoman, no matter what the facts, for gold? The answer was yes. And because their conduct was base, she felt at liberty to take whatever measures she could.

The windows in the dorm had no bars but neither were they the sash variety, and there would be a long drop from this second-floor lockup to the hard ground. The dormitory door was always locked, and inmates who could walk were taken to the dining area, a place of plain benches where they were fed cheap food, usually gruel of one sort or another, and something from the garden.

She resolved to work in the garden if possible, not only for the exercise, but also to survey the whole establishment. The more she saw from the outside of the structures, the more she would know about means to escape.

The prescribed way of addressing Mrs. Botts to gain her attention was to raise a hand and wait, and maybe she would attend you, maybe not. So when the matron next entered the ward, March raised an arm and waved it. Mrs. Botts approached like a steamboat and then settled a wary step or two away, lest the madwoman leap at her throat.

"I see there is a garden, madam. I like gardening. I am good at it. With your permission, I would like to hoe and weed and water."

The behemoth eyed her coldly. "They all say that," she said. "They see the garden and think they'll just walk away. We have a remedy for that. Hobbles. If you wish to garden, we'll allow it, but you'll be shackled. And if you plan on killing anyone with a hoe or a rake, you'll discover the discipline of the whip."

That certainly wasn't what March had expected, but she didn't hesitate.

"I'll garden, and observe your boundaries," she said.

The blue-eyed Botts grunted, making no reply. Then she wheeled away, without deciding the issue.

This might be an asylum, but it was not a friendly one.

The woman hunched in the next bunk caught

her attention. She wore a scarf, had weepy eyes, reddish flesh, and thinning hair.

"I'm March McPhee."

"*Brottslig*," she said.

"Ah, is that your name?"

"*Bry sig om*," she said.

So that was it. The woman couldn't speak a word of English. She seemed desperately lonely and maybe that was the reason. Or worse, maybe that was why she had been committed to this place. An asylum would be a good place to get rid of someone who couldn't defend herself.

March tried to talk to the woman, and the woman tried to talk to her, but the best March could do was assume that the woman was Scandinavian. Which country, she didn't know. And why she was in Warm Springs would always be a mystery. But there she was, tiny, forgotten, desolate.

After a few stabs at it, March reached over and patted the woman on the arm. The little creature caught March's hand and held it tight, her grip warm and desperate. March let it all play out, the woman gripping her hand, until at last she needed to move about, and pulled her hand free. The woman cried out, reached for March, and then fell back, tears welling up on her reddened face. The woman's small hands clenched and unclenched.

"I will be back to talk with you," March said. "Somehow."

The hours passed slowly. March fought back despair, the underlying knowledge that she had been wrongfully adjudged insane, confined for life, and there was not a soul on earth who might help her.

She quietly surveyed the inmates. They varied widely, from seamed old women to weeping young ones. Some wore leather restraints, the purpose of which she could only surmise, but they apparently were intended to keep the women from damaging themselves. The saddest case was a woman whose arms were pinned together.

March tried to talk to them all, but some were incoherent or silent, while others broke into litanies of grief or anger. Some made perfect sense; others began stories of heartache or persecution or hatred. It all made March wonder about those confined for criminal insanity, ones who would kill or rape or torture or commit suicide if they ever broke free. Surely this asylum served a valid purpose; the trouble was, some of the inmates plainly were not insane, but had been committed merely to get rid of them.

There was no lunch. The inmates were fed twice a day, herded into a dining area and handed a bowl and a spoon. Except that some were denied a spoon, and had to lift the bowl to consume whatever was in it, which was usually a pallid stew. Variety mattered little; what good would it do among the mad?

A week slid by, and March was restless. She had not yet been allowed to garden. She scarcely knew what lay outside of the doors of the building, or what her chances would be to slip away. If anything characterized this place, it was the oppressive sameness of each day, each hour, each week. She stood before the windows, memorizing every distant ridge, the river bottoms, the weather. No wonder they could catch runaways so easily. The land hid little; any dog could scout out a runaway in a few hours.

The matron and her small staff rarely entered the ward, and often contented themselves with a quick survey of the inmates to see what might be amiss. This was a place shot with dullness. Even the desperation of some of the women was dull because it never varied, never ended. Conversation was a rarity; some couldn't manage it, while others didn't know English, and others had slid into utter silence.

Then one day the matron appeared, nodded to March, took her down creaking wooden stairs, and out the doors to the generous gardens.

"You wanted it, you can have it," she said. "But you'll be in hobbles. Just don't get notions." She paused. "Some inmates want to destroy the crops, hoe them down. If you try that, you'll end your chance to work here."

A sleepy male orderly appeared, carrying some cruel contrivance, and soon March was wearing a device that wrapped around both calves and couldn't be unbuckled without a special tool inserted into a little slot. Her task was to hoe and weed rows of beans. There were half a dozen other inmates at work, all men. All hobbled. An overseer did nothing but sit in a lawn chair and watch.

She set to work. The garden was a great success. Rows of healthy vegetables filled several acres. She worked quietly down the rows, whacking away weeds, working steadily until she tired. There was no Simon Legree with a whip. When she wearied, she walked as best she could with the hobbles to a pail where there was water and a cup, and slaked her thirst. It was during those moments that she studied the sleepy asylum, watched tradesmen arrive with supplies and then turn their wagons toward Anaconda. Maybe one of them would carry her away, under a tarpaulin, to the nearby smelter town run by the Anaconda Copper Mining Company. Maybe the best flight would be straight into the neighboring city.

But she had come to realize that the very clothing she wore, a plain gray Mother Hubbard dress, was a sign of her incarceration, and would immediately alert an observer. Still, she toiled at her hoeing, studied the entire asylum, and hoped to learn how to put wings on her shoulders and fly away.

She liked the hoeing and gardening. Each day an

orderly came for her, escorted her to the extensive garden, put her in hobbles, and left her to her toil. She was permitted to work at her own pace, rest when she needed to, pause for a drink of water, and even converse with other inmates, if they were working adjacent rows. Sometimes they hoed and weeded; once they bucketed water when summer heat threatened the crops; and now and then they harvested their produce. Beans, squash, cucumbers, zucchini, and later, tomatoes. The hills of potatoes were coming along.

And still she studied the way things worked. The employment shifts. The endless wagons of suppliers. The asylum ate firewood in its cookstoves, and its potbellied stoves in the dormitories, and as fall approached, yards of cordwood grew near the service areas of the asylum.

Then one day a firewood deliveryman with a ruddy face caught her as she rested.

"You wouldn't be March McPhee, would you?"

She stared, amazed, into the blank face of a stranger, and then nodded.

"Tipperary's been looking for you."

"Oh, oh, oh . . ."

"Seems a loose-tongued patron began talking, and a barkeep always listens."

She stared about wildly, fearing trouble, but the day was progressing serenely.

"Be ready tomorrow. I'll be driving the wood

wagon. It's got a tarpaulin, and a fresh bright dress under, and you'll be changing."

"But these hobbles!"

"We've been studying on it." He waved a slim metal pick. "This is the latchkey. I'll leave it with you. You've watched it done a hundred times. Only tomorrow, you'll do it yourself."

TWENTY-ONE

He was there. Loading cordwood into the woodyard that sleepy morning while the air was cool and fresh and the day barely begun. Her task that day was to hoe the potatoes, where weeds were threatening to overrun the hills. She was the first out; other gardeners would drift in later.

He strode purposefully to her, and she feared someone might be watching. But the asylum was still barely stirring.

He smiled. "In the toolshed is a carpetbag. In it is men's clothing. Britches, shirt, straw hat, a red bandanna to wear about your neck. Hide that hair. Put it on. Put your women's things in the carpetbag, and your hobble. You have the pick?"

She nodded.

"When you come out, put the carpetbag in the wagon and help me unload the cordwood. When we're done, we'll drive away."

"Just like that?"

"We planned it best we could. There are no armed guards. This is an asylum, not a jail."

He returned to his task, unloading stick after stick of pine for the potbellied woodstoves and the cookstove. Her heart raced. She slid in, first surveying the quiet grounds, knowing it would take time to make the change. And then she pushed the pick into the hobbles and each leather contraption fell free. She yanked the clothing from the carpetbag and swiftly filled it with her own and the hobble, and wished she had a looking glass to see whether she looked like a male. She pushed her red hair under the floppy hat, and tied the bandanna, hoping to hide her neck, and then stepped out. She was just in time. One of the male inmates was heading for the shed to collect his tools. The old man ignored her.

She strode toward the woodlot, trembling, and soon was lifting cordwood and stacking it in orderly rows.

He winked. The wink told her to relax; it was all a lark.

But she couldn't relax, and worked furiously, wanting to speed time along, faster and faster. And then it was done.

"You drive," he said.

"I've only done it a little."

He just grinned, and settled beside her on the wagon seat. She flapped the lines over the croup of the dray, and the old horse took off handsomely, trotting away, the wagon wheels rolling, the wagon lurching beneath her.

"Well, lass, we fetched you," he said. "I'm Mack. Call me whatever name pleases you."

"Oh, Mack. You and Tip and all your friends."

"We fetched you out."

"It's not over."

"No, but for now, just steer the nag along, and we'll have a little chat as we go. We've a two-hour drive to Anaconda, so there's no sense in wearing out the dray."

"But I want to know everything!"

She peered behind her, fearful of being followed, but the morning sun shone quietly over empty plains, and the asylum dwindled down and finally slid from the horizon.

"It was on our minds, you disappearing from the little washerwoman cottage, and no one at Tipperary's had the faintest idea what happened. Maybe you'd gone away. But it worried us some, day after day. We'd made you our charge, and then you weren't there, and many a boyo didn't feel right about it. We put out feelers. Maybe you were up in the mountains, the way you had been.

"Then one of Tip's customers, Jerusalem Jones, he of the funeral parlor, he gossips a little, and Tip serves him another rye, and he talks and hints a little more, and never quite saying where the lady went, and then Jerusalem, he spills it. She's been locked away, he says, smirking. She's gone for good.

"But we didn't know where or how. Who or what. But some things get put on the record, like inmates to the county jail, and certain district court records we got a peek at, and we got the whole picture. You'd been railroaded right into the place where you'd be stuck the rest of your life, not to mention that anything you said or swore or wrote would be discounted. That was a fine old place for the widow, and that's how we got the word."

She felt like kissing him.

"But it took some scheming and a little arguing and a vote among us. And a little money for rail tickets. And a day or two of hanging about there, seeing how it all went. And looking at you with a field glass, seeing it was really you. It was."

"Where are we going?"

"Anaconda. See the works, on that hill, and that big stack? That's Marcus Daly's copper smelter, biggest in the world, and that's his town, right down to the street names. We're going there."

"But what if they catch us?"

"We'll turn you into the lady you always was," Mack said. "If you want, pull that tarp back and look."

She stood, worked her way back into the wagon bed, lifted the tarp, and discovered a pink dress, a hat loaded with straw flowers, white gloves, a pair of white shoes, and a lady's handbag.

"I'll busy myself with the driving," he said, smiling slightly.

"The shoes. What if they don't fit?"

"They're yours. The ones in the washerwoman cottage. We whited them up real ladylike."

The thought of changing clothing out in the wide open, behind this man's back, dismayed her, but then she did it. He was most respectful, studying crows and magpies and hawks and talking to his dray. She was half wild to complete the task, her eye sharp on every horizon, ready to dive under the tarpaulin. And yet nothing at all disturbed the morning, a quiet drive down a lonely road, the birds trilling.

She stuffed the men's clothing into the carpet-bag, which was brimming now with disguises. And then she clambered over the bench, and sat down.

A sideways glance assured Mack, and he swung around to eye her.

"A blooming lady," he said.

"Running off with a true gentleman," she said, admiring the compact man who was nonchalantly shepherding her through a great escape. And still the horizon was not disturbed by the passage of man or beast.

"What's your story, may I ask?"

"Story?"

"You need a story. A man with a badge rides up, what do you say?"

"I'll tell him to mind his bloody business."

Mack smiled. "That's good. Don't tangle yourself with a lot of malarkey. If he asks what a lady's doing on a cordwood wagon, don't give him a clue." He leaned toward her. "I'm from the old country, County Cork, and I know about these things. Best just don't say anything."

"And you're helping a Scot?"

"We have a thing in common. I'll say it plain. That clan, the Roaches, have a mission of their own. To stop Irish immigration. Once, they even tried to steal Tommy Cruse's Drumlummon from him. They used to be the Know Nothings, keep the Irish and Germans and Catholics out of the United States. Now they have no name, but it's the same. Keep the Irish out." He eyed her. "Some of us at Tip's, we're Fenians. The brotherhood. Keep that under your hat."

Ahead a way rose Mount Haggin, and at its foot lay a shining city, and off to the left, a great industrial complex, with a towering stack pumping white smoke into the blue skies. She watched it loom larger and larger as the wagon approached. They began to meet other wagons and buggies on the outskirts.

"What happens next?" she asked. "I'm entirely in your hands, I believe."

"Well, we've been wrestling with it. There's tickets for you clear to Marysville if you want them. The Butte, Anaconda and Pacific, that'll take you to Butte. The Great Northern to Helena. And the Northern Pacific to Marysville. But is it what you want, lady? You'd be swiftly recognized in Marysville."

So it was back to her. That was good, she thought, even as she wished someone would be her champion and right the wrongs and free her.

"If they catch me, they'll send me back there," she said. "And lock me up."

"That's true. But maybe you could change your name, live somewhere else."

"I could run away," she said. "Why go back to Marysville?"

He slid into silence, and steered his dray toward a woodcutter's yard on the north edge of town. Heaps of tree trunks and limbs lay about. A rotary saw powered by a donkey steam engine stood silent.

"But I won't. I will see it through, win or lose. What's life for, anyway? To run away?"

"You won't be alone," he said, and she heard approval in his voice.

"Is the washerwoman cottage still there for me?"

"It is. They know nothing of this. But Constable Roach, he'll be looking for you as soon as he learns about this."

"I don't know what I'll do, but I'm going to try," she said. "Tell me about the mine."

He withdrew a pocket watch. "Ma'am, the station's a long hike from this woodlot, and the Butte train, she'll be boarding passengers right now and leaving in ten minutes. Here's your tickets if it pleases you. Next train's not till late."

Mack handed her an envelope.

"Oh, Mack," she said. "Oh, Mack."

He pulled off his cap and smiled. And handed

her the carpetbag. And pointed toward a white station two blocks distant or so.

"Oh, Mack," she said, and hastened toward the building.

That was the last she saw of the man who had plucked her free.

She hurried, almost feverish to escape, and raced onto the platform just as a blue-clad conductor was lifting the steel step stool. He saw her, helped her up, and she found herself in a dark coach, mostly empty, with a ticket, not one cent, and a bag full of odd clothing.

She had hardly settled in a wine-colored horsehair seat before she felt the lurch, heard the hiss of steam, and felt the car roll toward Butte. She dug into the envelope, found the right ticket, a yellow square attached to other yellow squares. When the conductor came, she was ready.

She was free. A woman alone. The world was not watching her. The landscape passing across the window was gentle, anonymous, browning in late summer sun, and still virgin. The Territory was barely settled.

She smelled Butte before she saw it, as acrid fumes from mine boilers and mills eddied through the coach. Off to her left, the ramshackle city climbed a grade, and headframes from its many mines peppered the top. She saw not a tree, and had heard that the arsenic in the smoke extinguished plant life, if not animal. This was the fiefdom of the Anaconda Copper Mining Company, and it was worth far more than any gold mine ever known. She didn't care for it, at least what she could see. It was a cancer growing out of the wilderness. Eventually, the train squealed to a halt at the clapboard terminal of the little railroad built by the copper king Marcus Daly, and she found herself stepping down to a gravel platform, wondering where to go next. Or if she could go somewhere. That was always a livelihood in Butte, she had heard.

She found a ticket window in the spare little station, and presented her ticket there.

"I'm booked for Helena, and don't know where to go."

"Stay right here. Great Northern, leaves at four forty-five."

That was a long wait. Her stomach was growling. She hadn't a nickel. And once she got to Helena, she still had to catch the one-a-day train to Marysville. She was hungry and a long way from home.

She settled into one of the polished benches in the waiting room, the ones that looked like pews where people could worship the railway gods. At least there was a drinking fountain. She could quench her thirst. But it was going to be a long wait.

A man in a dust cap approached, pulled it from

his head, and stood before her. She was suddenly wary.

"Mrs. McPhee?" he asked.

She refused to acknowledge it. "You have the wrong person, I'm afraid."

He looked uncomfortable. "Tip says to fetch you a dinner and see to your comfort."

"Tip? Tip?"

"Tipperary Leary, madam. He'll be very glad when I wire him. We've been waiting. We've been hoping."

He smiled. She arose, gratefully. But she couldn't help but stare, at the man, at the others in the station, at the people on the platform. At anyone who might show her a badge and drag her back to the asylum for the insane.

"I'm Sean," he said. "Come this way."

TWENTY-TWO

His name was Sean Touhy, and he led her to a bench and handed her something wrapped in butcher paper, and an apple.

"She's a pasty," he said.

She stared blankly.

"A meat pie, with a little patooties and spices, in a pastry shell. We take them down, and they make our lunch."

She peeled back the paper and discovered a warm and fragrant pastry. She bit in, discovering beef and potato and other things she couldn't identify, and juices still warm, and a high flavor that she enjoyed. She ate another bite, and another, and wolfed several more, while he watched, approving.

"I'm a mucker in the Neversweat, old Daly's mine. I came over about ten years ago from County Clare. They paid the way. I make a good living, send a little back, and live in the Big Ship—that's the rooming house for Daly's working men."

She wolfed the pasty as fast as she could eat, pushing aside any worries about digesting it half-chewed.

"They wire me, the brothers I mean, saying to look for you, lady in pink, so here I come. I'll sit with you, fetch whatever you need, and put you on the coach to Helena for sure, so you'll be going home."

"Well, Sean, you saved my life. I never was so starved! I don't know how to thank you, but I'll find a way."

She wiped her lips with the butcher paper, and disposed of it.

"They say the gang up there, ones called Laidlow group, they drove you out."

"I never know whether it's Laidlow or Roach, but it's all kin."

"I get word from the brothers, and I don't know about Helena," Sean said. "But if they say to help a lady in pink, and get something hearty into her, I'll do it, no questions asked, no favors wanted."

He was twitchy, and finally stood. "That train, it's number seven-thirty-two, and you ask the conductor or brakeman if it's the Helena train, and he'll wave you up. Me, I'm gonna be on shift pretty quick, so I'll let you be."

"Oh, Sean . . ."

"You're a pretty one," he said, and swiftly retreated. She watched him abandon the tan-colored station and trot up the long grade toward a cluster of mines with smoke boiling from a row of stacks.

She still had the apple. She would save it for Helena. She wondered if pasties could be had in Marysville. She thought they might. Tommy

Cruse had hired his own people, the way the mining men of Butte did.

This brotherhood, she knew little about it, but she knew it was a secret army working toward Irish independence. And for some reason they fought the Roaches and Laidlows, the whole clan of them. And that made her a friend.

She caught the train without difficulty, and sat in a old coach with wicker seats. Ahead was a baggage car, and that was it. The little train chuffed up a grade, and then wailed its way along an alpine valley clear to Helena. She watched nervously as the engine hissed to a stop, billowing steam. But she saw no sign of constables or trouble.

She had another long wait in Helena, and was grateful for the apple. Her handsome pink dress and silk-flowered hat proved to be disguise enough, so she walked the streets, up Last Chance Gulch, once a wild placer mining district, and now lined with small shops, and a few handsome stone buildings barely completed. She eyed the county courthouse on Broadway, where a crooked judge along with a crooked quack had banished her from the sight of the world—and had nearly brought her life to a sad limbo.

And it was not over. And she had no means. She was realizing she had friends, better friends than she had imagined, and maybe there was some hope in all that. She drifted to the little station down on the lower end of the gulch, and caught the right train, the one to Marysville, and arrived there at night.

There was no one waiting for her. Constable Roach wasn't lurking. The half dozen other passengers swiftly dissipated into the quiet. Up the slope, the Drumlummon stamp mill was throbbing, its heartbeat keeping the little town alive.

This was home. She walked to the washerwoman cottage in full dark, her carpetbag heavy, her arm aching. She was weary. She only wanted sleep, days and days of sleep. The night was peaceful. It was not late; the late summer sun had settled only two hours before. She did not know what she would do next, or how she would avoid recapture—surely Marysville would be the first place they would hunt for her—but this night she would sleep.

She found the cottage, sitting in its grove, quiet and serene, but she first circled it in the pale moonlight, and finally edged to the back window, and saw nothing. She entered through the laundry room, the door creaking, but nothing leapt out at her. And then she stepped into the one-room quarters. Nothing. Only the great quiet of a safe place, the pale glow of night filtering through the window.

On the sturdy table, in the moonlight, was a plate with some hard-boiled eggs, some pretzels, and several apples. She had friends, and they had not forgotten her, and they knew her needs. Never before had she contemplated the value of true friends.

"Tipperary Leary, you are a good man," she said.

A little food in her stomach was just fine. She ate, abandoned the pink dress that had protected her for many hours and miles, and stumbled into bed, her eyes suddenly wet. She wanted to think she was home, but her mind would not let her. At least it was not a narrow bed in a lunatic asylum. Or the metal bench of a prison cell.

She slept fitfully, and awakened to a soft tapping. She had no robe, but hurried into the asylum dress, the drab Mother Hubbard, and peered out.

"Tipperary!" she said, opening to him.

"So it is the madwoman," he said.

She could not answer, but hurried him to one of the two wooden chairs.

"Would you like an apple?" she asked, and they smiled.

"You are safe for the moment," he said. "But only that. They will expect you here, and spring upon you when they can. Tell me all, spare me nothing."

She did, beginning with her trip to Helena to confront District Judge Roach. When she got to the exam by Doctor Jerrold Laidlow, and the results, Tip Leary was hissing like a steam kettle.

"I knew nothing about him!" he said. "So that's how they railroaded you. Without a care about you, who you are, whether or not you're mad as a hatter. None of it. Just get rid of her, any way they could. And they did."

"I thought I was all alone, washed up on a beach in a strange land, until yesterday," she said.

Tip Leary didn't like that, and glared a moment. Then he reached across the table and took her hand. "You were never alone," he said. "And never will be."

She felt embarrassed. If there was one idea that dwelled in her thoughts after being condemned to spend all the rest of her life in an asylum, was that she was alone, forgotten, and beyond help. "Oh, Tip," she said.

"Now there's more, Mrs. McPhee."

"It's March, please."

He nodded. "They've expanded your mine. They've got two shifts, a dozen men, and the ore's thicker and better every time they blast. They're running laterals, it's becoming a big T in there, and the word is, they'll be taking out a thousand dollars' worth of ore every day. They're sinking some capital back in, with timbering, a dormitory, a tailings dump, and all. But they're running two shifts a day, every day, and your little mine's a bonanza mine, and even now, just at the start, it's clearing ten thousand a month, net profit. I hear that from all over. I hear it from Wittgenstein, from half a dozen people at the mill, where that ore goes. And, get this, from Jerusalem Jones, who comes in and brags about it. He's the big cheese now."

"A hundred thousand a year," she said. "Even after expenses. If it lasts."

"It's lasting. They say that seam follows a fault, and that fault's solid quartz full of gold, and it's now a yard wide and getting wider." He eyed her. "There's wagons up and down Long Gulch all day, every day," he said. "They go straight to the Drumlummon for custom milling. The Roach crowd's already got its first monthly payout. There's six principals, and a second generation, they get halves of one share. Maybe twenty. That boy Jerusalem, he comes into my place, and likes to brag. I sure do listen. He got his first half-share payment, and spent a lot of it on suds. He says there's to be one a month now."

"I have my work cut out for me," she said.

"You gonna fight?"

"You just persuaded me to."

"And you on the lam. You got any ideas?"

She did, but simply shook her head. She wasn't ready to say anything about that. "I'll need some help," she said. "Food. I don't have a shilling."

"Consider it done. It'll be here, on the table, whenever you come here. This place, it's fine for the moment, but if they start hunting you down, it's not safe here."

"I know of some places up high," she said. "Good until snow comes."

He grinned. "You are some lady," he said.

"There's something you could do," she said. "Who's in that clan? Who's getting paid? If Judge Roach gets a share, I want proof of it. If that miserable doctor, Jerrold Laidlow, gets a cut, I want to know it. If our Constable Roach gets a cut, I'd like proof of it."

"That's a tough clan, March. I don't know why I have a bad time calling you by your given name. They can pinch any man, convict a man, throw the man into jail, seize his assets."

"Women. Women too, Tip."

"And worse," he said. "When you've got the police and courts and a crooked doctor, you're a machine."

He slipped away, staying in the aspen grove until he was clear of the washerwoman cottage. She watched him cross open fields, and she saw no one eyeing him. It was time to plan her day; or rather, her night.

She had things to do. First, she needed to stow away her things. She would stay here off and on, meet Tip here, pick up supplies here, but she wanted the place to seem unoccupied to any casual observer. And she feared that soon there would be not-very-casual observers.

She put on the men's clothing that she wore out of the asylum. It was dark; the britches fit, and it would take some scuffing. Then she stored most everything else, including the pink dress and hat, in a closet. She put a few things, mostly food, in the carpetbag; those would go with her. She debated taking the men's straw hat, and decided she would even though it was light colored and visible. But it hid her hair.

When she was ready, she locked the door behind her, studied the quiet world, the long limbs of the mountains, the distant town of Marysville, and then headed across open country, far from anyone, heading quietly toward Long Gulch and the dangerous trip toward her mine.

She entered the gulch as if stepping into a narrowing funnel, knowing that if she encountered one of those many ore wagons, she might have no place to hide. But for the first hour she met no one, and when she did see a heavy wagon coming down from the mine, drawn by a six-mule team, she had no trouble slipping into a rocky defile choked with brush, and the wagon rumbled by. That was close to where she intended to leave the gulch anyway, and so she started climbing the timbered slopes, negotiating her way around deadfall and ledges. She saw no one now; the woods shaded and closeted her, and she slipped through as lightly as a doe, heading for the vaulting cliffs and scree not far from her mine.

She spotted no one; no one saw her. She reached her hideaway and found it untouched, except perhaps by animals. She found nothing that suggested the miners nearby had located it.

She settled in, and then climbed toward another overhang to the left, even higher, making sure that Kermit's supplies were where she had hidden them long before.

They were all present. The Bickford fuse, the copper caps, the crimping tool, the lamps and igniters, and the box of waxy red DuPont dynamite.

TWENTY-THREE

March marveled. The McPhee Mine was large and busy. From her vantage point, shadowed by forest, she noted that large stacks of timbers waited to be taken into the mine. Shiny rails erupted from the mine head and ended on a low trestle where one-ton ore cars could unload rock into a growing tailings heap at one point, or into ore wagons at another spot. She saw two steep-sided wagons, with their teams, awaiting loads to haul to Marysville. Just outside of the portal, two sorters separated quartz and country rock in mixed loads. Timber men were shaping posts and cross-pieces, and sending them into the mine on empty ore cars.

The powdermen were using Kermit's powder safe, located well to one side of the shaft. Even as she watched, two muckers hand-pushing an ore car appeared at the portal and the surface men took over. The muckers rolled another car into the gloom. She saw Jerusalem Jones, apparently the straw boss, wandering about, a sidearm prominent at his hip. She backed away, slipped into the welcoming forest, and headed for another vantage point a hundred yards lower. Her canvas house had vanished, and in its place stood a crude, tarpaper barracks, the paper held onto rough lumber with battens. The remote mine had crews on hand at all times.

A bell clanged and three burly miners, wearing dust caps, slowly emerged from the portal, blinking at the bright sun after hours in deep dark.

"Fire in the hole," yelled a powderman, walking deliberately out of the portal, and turning sharply left. Several miners stood well away, and a few seconds later a muffled rumble broke loose, a burst of dirty air boiled out, followed by several more thuds, and then silence. That would keep the next shift busy. And if this mine was true to form, the second shift would start an hour later, after the choking dust had mostly settled. No one was collecting at the portal just yet.

She had been watching much of the afternoon, getting a sense of how the McPhee was being run. Every carload of milky quartz that tumbled into a freight wagon sent a pang through her. That was her gold. She waited patiently, watching a red squirrel hide pine nuts against the looming winter. The next shift collected only a half hour later, but this shaft was still very short, and the blast had actually blown much of the dust and debris out of the portal. She reckoned that the second shift would finish up at midnight. It would be working the other lateral, not the one that had just been blown. Under the lamps, or candles, the muckers would shovel ore or country rock into cars. If they had laid a turning sheet on the floor ahead of the blast, the rock would have landed on sheet iron, making the shoveling much easier, and making it possible for someone to turn an ore car around and back onto its rails.

It was impressive. They were taking several tons of rock a day out of that portal. They were running three or four ore wagons down to the mill, for custom processing, every day, including Sundays.

Probably at midnight the second shift would finish, the powdermen would fire a charge in the face of the other lateral, and the mine would rest quiet and dark until before dawn, when the morning shift would start in all over again. That quiet time was what she was waiting for.

She had seen what she needed to. But she hovered patiently, feeling the cool evening air slide down the slope and eddy through the forest. The season would change soon, and the freedom of summer would give way to cold rains, snow, and struggle. She watched the crew straggle back to the tarpaper barracks. A stovepipe in the roof leaking white smoke told her that someone was cooking. It would be a rough life, breaking up the bitter rock, shoveling tons of it, breathing the flinty, gritty air lingering in the shaft and laterals. It was a grim labor for these womanless men.

She saw no sign of Jerusalem Jones now, and surmised that he rode to town each evening and showed up only during the day. That was good. She saw no dog, and that was good. A barking dog would be the last thing she wanted. One of the men emerged from the shack, headed to an odorous place, and drained himself. Maybe that was good, too. She needed to know what sort of traffic the night might bring.

She was cold and weary, still worn from her escape. But the sooner she did what she must do, the better. She slipped through the forest in last light. She could see twilight through the treetops, but it was night in the forest. She paused at her hideaway, which seemed cold and uncomfortable in the changing climate. But it would shelter her now. She collected Kermit's DuPont Giant Powder, waxy red cylinders of dynamite, which was simply blasting oil, nitroglycerin, mixed with fine clay to stabilize it.

She had a dozen sticks, not very much for the task at hand, but it would have to do. At the back of the walled-off overhang, she lit a carbide lamp. It hissed quietly, popped, and threw ghostly light around her shelter. She had watched Kermit perform the next steps—he had crossly urged her to leave—and everything she did now would be modeled on what she had seen. She was preparing two bundles of dynamite which she intended to ignite at the faulted area that had doomed Kermit. That was the only spot in the shaft where loose dynamite might do some serious work. The badly faulted area was about fifty feet in. She would need three feet of Bickford fuse, which burned thirty seconds to the foot. The rule was to walk, not run. Runners stumbled and fell and perished. She cut the three feet and picked up a copper fulminate of mercury blasting cap, and gently slid the fuse into the copper tube, and carefully crimped the fuse tight, using Kermit's special crimping tool as gently as she knew how. The spark burning up the center of the corded fuse would need to reach the fulminate. That would ignite the cap. The cap would ignite the stable dynamite.

Her pulse climbed.

She gently sliced open one red stick of the DuPont, and eased the cap into the soft giant powder, as it was called, and carefully wrapped a thin wire around the fused stick, holding the fuse tight. Now she had a very dangerous primed charge of dynamite. She gathered five more sticks around the primed one, and wrapped wire around them, completing one bundle. She peered outside, saw that there was an alpenglow that would light the way, and carefully carried the bundle down to the mine, placing it behind some rock. She eased up to her hideaway even as the last glow faded into night, stumbling now and then.

The second shift was hard at work, but no one was outside. Shifting light from carbide lamps bled from the mine portal. It was too dark to do anything except work on the face within, the men double jacking holes into the face and filling them with DuPont sticks just like hers. Apparently this smaller group simply drilled and loaded charges and blew them, and went to bed. In the morning, the muckers would start shoveling ore from each lateral.

She understood the way things worked at the McPhee.

The stumbles were a warning, and she heeded it. She would not charge the second bundle. Instead, she put the remaining sticks back, returned the caps to a separate notch in the cliff, and stowed the rest. Now she would wait. She tried lying against the hard stone, but it hurt her cruelly. Even the stern little bunk at the asylum brought more comfort than this.

Would they come looking for her? Most certainly. They would find this place. She would leave nothing here. She thought the remaining explosives would be safe in their niche in the cliff well above, invisible unless one stumbled on the little hollow. She would leave them. She was wearing black pants and a blue chambray shirt, and only her straw hat and pale face might give her away. She thought to abandon the hat. It was a man's hat, and she would leave it there, for the searchers to find.

Time stretched slowly, and now the night was

cold. When she judged the time to be about midnight, she eased down the slope, gingerly crossing the talus that slid from above, and made her way to the mine. It glowed in the white light of a quarter moon. She waited, wary of a sentry, but saw nothing. There was no reason for the miners to post a sentry; they simply had folded for the night. She stood at the dark mouth of the mine, peering into the gloom. She saw no shifting lights, no sign of work. She eased in, her passage lit by moonlight, her eyes sharp in the deep gloom. She wasn't sure at first where the dangerous area was, the loose and splintered rock that had killed Kermit. But then she knew. It was where the timbering began. The first fifty feet remained without support except at the mouth, where timbers protected against loose surface rock.

She couldn't see the lagging, the heavy planks resting on the crossbeams to catch any caving stone. She also couldn't see what space existed above the lagging, space where she intended to place her charge. She would briefly need to light a lamp to see what she was doing, and could only hope no one down below would see the light.

She chose a candle in a reflective holder, something she could blow out in an instant. Kermit had mostly used lamps, but he kept a few candles handy. Quietly, she plunged into the gloom, reached the point where the timbering began, and lit the candle. She studied the lagging, and the rough space above it. She wasn't tall enough to see what lay above, and she wondered whether she should wait until she could know where to place the charge.

She felt herself being watched, turned, and found two small eyes, bright buttons of light, near the portal. Some wild creature. It ambled off. Skunk, badger, marmot, raccoon, who could say? She retreated from the shaft, worked her way around equipment, and reached the spot where her charge rested. Six sticks, primed and ready.

She wondered if they would be effective. Dynamite worked best when confined by solid rock. Miners even plugged the charge with a little muck to increase the explosive force. But her charge would rest on thick planks under the unstable faulted area, and not even six sticks could equal the force of a charge resting inside solid rock. But she had learned a few things, and one of them was that unstable areas followed their own rules. A low-level blast could trigger a landslide.

That was her hope.

Gingerly she carried the charge into the portal, and worked through the gloom, found the timbering, and reached upward. She slid the charge into the few inches of space and eased it as far as her arm could push. She felt the fuse, the rat-tail, hang from the lagging, ready to ignite.

She was a little shaky. A charge that could ignite from a sharp blow, and could blow her to bits, did not induce calm in her.

"Well, Kermit," she said aloud, "I'm ready. This is where you fell. This is where our fate is sealed."

She heard nothing, but thought he was there, listening, smiling.

Now she needed another sort of courage, the will to walk out, not run, because if she panicked and fell, she might never again see a sunrise.

She scratched a match, watched it flare, found the fuse dangling from above, but the match died. She caught the fuse in her hand and scratched another match to life. Powdermen did not use matches. They held a flame to the fuse until they were sure it was spitting sparks. That match expired, so she tried the candle, getting a flame going, and then, her hands trembling, holding the steady flame to the fuse. In a moment she saw sparks, heard it hiss, and she knew she had ninety seconds to vacate the mine and turn away from the portal and the powerful blast that would erupt from it.

She walked. In fact, walking proved to be easier than lighting the fuse. She walked carefully, the fuse spitting behind her, walked toward the open night ahead, walked step by step, walked into the starlit night, turned sharply right, kept on walking through the night, wondering when,

when, when, and then as she reached the edge of the little plateau, the earth bucked under her, and a throaty boom rumbled through the night, and the peace of the mountains was ruptured.

She could not see the result. She could only hope that the charge would trigger a landslide, and the unstable area would seal up the shaft for a long time. And keep them from stealing any more of her gold.

She threaded into the deep forest, when all she could see was the open sky, found her carpetbag just where she had left it, and hurried through the forest, her gaze uncanny, hastening down to Long Gulch, because she knew if she tarried, it would be sealed off and she might be trapped.

She exulted. She had begun to fight back, and this was a first step.

TWENTY-FOUR

Tipperary Leary brought her some papers. The *Helena Herald* said it loudest:

MADWOMAN ESCAPES FROM WARM SPRINGS

But the story was helpful. It described her as short, stout, and dark-haired. That offended her until she realized it was wrong on two counts: she had chestnut hair and had lost weight. Even better, it said she spoke with an Irish burr, and left behind a note threatening suicide. Officials were walking the Clark Fork River in search of a body.

"Suicide, Tip?"

"Our man Mack did a little more than he told you about," Tip said. "He left a note in the toolshed where you changed into pants. It said you despaired of life. They think you simply walked away."

March could scarcely believe her good fortune.

"Not to say they haven't looked here," Tip said. "Constable Roach. That cabal doesn't like the thought of you loose."

"Well, they must know. After I set the charge."

"They're not sure. They found a man's straw hat nearby. But they think it might be you."

"How far along are they?"

"They'll have it cleared in a few days. It's a narrow shaft, and only two men at a time can muck out that pile of rock. They've laid off half a dozen until they can reopen."

"Did it seal the shaft?"

"No, they could crawl over the top of the heap into the mine, that's what Jerusalem Jones said, vowing to catch and hang whoever did it. He's bragging that they'll have it up and running again in record time, and they'll find the pig who fired that charge."

"It's a good thing he stops in for a drink, Tip."

"I pour him one on the house now and then."

"Tip, why do you do this for me, you and your friends?"

He hesitated. "We have our reasons."

"Not we—you."

"Ladies deserve respect," he said, in a way that foreclosed further questions.

Tip had been faithful to his word. Each day, some fresh food appeared on the table of the washerwoman's cottage. That had sustained her for several days. Once she got into the handsome pink dress and silk-flower hat, and ventured into town, unchallenged, and mostly unobserved. New faces were routine in a bustling town.

Still, it was a risky thing, and she dreaded an encounter with Constable Roach, pink dress or not. But she was alone, and she felt a need to reconnect, to be among people, and not be hiding, or venturing out in disguise.

The weather was turning. Some fall rains had swept through, and people were burning cord-wood in their stoves again. One morning there was a veil of white on the peaks. It vanished later, but it was a sign of what would soon come to Marysville.

That night she slipped into her men's britches and blue shirt, and added a drab sweater that once had been Kermit's, and slipped into a cold wind, made her way up Long Gulch in darkness, and cut into the forest at about the right place. She was numb from the raw wind, but kept on until she could view the mine. It was dark. She circled down to the lower flat, with its tarpaper barracks, and peeked in through a grimy window. It was empty. On a mean night, they had all gone to town. But there was no lamp lit in the dormitory. She wasn't sure it had been vacated, and there was only one way to find out, so she opened the door noisily, yelled in a low voice, and aroused no one. She spotted a kerosene lamp, which was perfect. She unscrewed the wick, poured the kerosene onto the wood floor and walls nearest the stove, lit it, and backed away as flames licked up the walls closest to the potbellied stove. Then she headed into the night, an invisible wraith in dark colors, and made it back to Marysville even as the sky behind her was, for a little while, aglow with orange light.

That would slow them down some more. The nights were getting cold. They needed shelter now.

She padded back to Marysville, knowing that the barracks fire would trigger another, fiercer manhunt, and no building would go unexamined. The Roach crowd wouldn't for an instant believe it was accidental. The washerwoman cottage would not shelter her for long. And now the weather in that mountain locale could turn any day.

The next nights she dressed in dark clothing and probed the sprawling Drumlummon works, which clung to a hillside and covered many acres. Even as the night shift toiled, and ore cars were shunted from the mine to the mill, she examined every structure hoping to find a safe haven if she needed one. But she found nothing. There were sheds but they leaked air and were filled with kegs and crates.

"Arson!" screamed the headline of the Marysville weekly. "Madwoman on the Loose."

The paper said that Constable Roach was doing a door-to-door hunt for a woman believed to have escaped a Territorial asylum.

It was only a matter of time before they found her. What chance did she have?

Tipperary showed up one frosty dawn, knocking gently. She peeked out, and opened to him. He slipped in, carrying something.

"Cold in here," he said.

"I can no longer keep a fire."

He nodded.

"If I could get to Helena, find work—chambermaid, something . . . I've got to start somewhere else. Tip, I'm not making headway here."

"Well, look at this first, if you will."

He laid a gray-and-red clothbound ledger book on the table. The light was so low she could barely see what was written on its pages.

"This little book, it's your ticket. It's the Laidlow Group's accounting. It lists who's in on it, who's got a full share, who's got a half share—the younger ones have halves. It lists the whole blooming lot: Judge Roach in Helena, the constable here, the miserable doctor in Helena, his brother in the funeral home here. There's a page for Jerusalem Jones, a sister's son, who has half a share. He's the one who told me. He sat in my place, soaking up gin, and began telling me about this here ledger, and how it was kept at the funeral parlor, and how it showed the monthly accounting, and the payouts, not only from your mine, but all sorts of other properties and real estate they've gotten by rook and crook. Here it is, black-and-white, or blue-and-white, anyway, neat columns, sums piled up nice and even."

"And how did you get this?"

"Now there's a mystery, Mrs. McPhee. Some say it walked out the door and into my lap, like a yapping dog."

"Do they know it's missing?"

"So far, misplaced. In fact Jerusalem said so. They don't see it as a problem. Just a ledger that fell into the couch cushions or something."

"I wouldn't know what to do with it. And it's stolen."

Tipperary sighed. "It says here, Judge Roach, selfsame gent who shipped you to Warm Springs, got a payment from the McPhee. And Jerrold Laidlow, sort of an MD if you stretch his diploma a bit, the selfsame who found you mad as a hatter, he got his payment from the McPhee. And Laidlow himself, him who piled up your debt burying your man, and used it to steal a mine from you, he got his monthly dividend from your mine, after his cousin the judge euchred you out of the mine. I'd say, March McPhee, you've got the goods right here."

"Maybe I do. But what good will it do?"

"You might talk to a good, ethical, upstanding, honest, bold attorney, shaped a little like your friend Hermes Apollo, a man of forthright and honest greed."

"And other appetites," she added.

She wanted to like all this, but she couldn't. "This should be returned," she said.

"Oh, it will. It's just been borrowed—and copied."

"I'll talk to Hermes Apollo. You know, Tip, he's an oddly honest man. He puts his worst foot forward, and it's his way of being ethical. He's saying, here I am at my least noble."

"I'd need a few drinks down me before I could do that."

She smiled.

"This'll be found in the funeral home, lying on the floor, where it had been overlooked. But we'll have a fine copy, thanks to Mike Boyle, an accountant up to the mine. It sure is an interesting little ledger, eh?"

She clasped his hands. "I don't know what I'd do without you," she said.

Midday, she donned her handsome pink dress and flower-bedecked hat, and sallied out, hoping not to run across Constable Roach. It was a fine autumnal day, with a fresh breeze driving away the smoke from the mill boilers. She spotted the blue uniform on the other side of the street, but he took no notice of her. The pink dress had served its purpose, at least for the moment.

She found the attorney in his ornate Second Street chambers. He peered up, surprised, slowly registering her garb.

"Fancy that," he said. "The madwoman herself. What have you done?"

It took a while, but she laid it out for him, while his eyebrows caterpillared up and down and his fingers harmonized on the polished table.

"I can't do much with stolen evidence," he said.

"The ledger's gone back to the funeral home."

"I can't do much with stolen information. They will ask where it came from, and any court would throw it out." But he gazed into space a while. "But there are always ways. A civil suit. A subpoena of the ledger, necessary evidence. We'll demand it. We'll threaten dire things if we don't see it and admit it as evidence. It would be in another district court, of course. Judge Roach's a defendant. The dockets are crowded so it'll take a year. I'll seek an injunction that would stop the mining until ownership is settled. We're in for the long haul. So, I do this, and what happens to you? You're a fugitive, are you not?"

"I thought you'd prove that Dr. Laidlow's a quack."

"That might not bail you out. Once a mad-woman, always a madwoman. And what if I lose the case? You're bucking the most powerful cabal in the Territory."

She had no answer to that.

Then he seemed to light up. That was the thing about Hermes Apollo. You could watch energy flow in and out of him. He would inflate, his eyes would brighten, or he would deflate like a tired hot-air balloon. Just now he was expanding.

"How are you going to pay me? I am a very expensive lawyer," he said. "I really don't like to work on a contingency fee—payment contingent on success. No, that's a fool's game."

"With profits from the mine once I get it back. I'll pay you well and fast."

He sighed. "Your word is splendid, Mrs. McPhee,

but all the best intentions in the world can't keep things from going awry. There's many a slip twixt the cup and the lip, as the saying goes. Now, here's how we'll do it. If I win, I shall possess half the McPhee Mine, plus one percent so I have control. If I lose—well, you shall marry me, like it or not."

"What?"

"If we lose, madam, they will promptly send you back to Warm Springs, since the court will have confirmed that you are a madwoman. But if you should marry me promptly, then I have custody, you see. The madwoman's in her husband's custody."

"Custody, custody?"

"Of the madwoman. A husband has that power. It wouldn't be so bad, dear lady. Endure my goatish behavior, endure my occasional naughtiness, for which the god Apollo is famous, and you will live your life in perfect liberty the other ninety-eight percent of your time. You'll be a prominent woman in Marysville society."

She took a deep breath. "Is this a proposition or a proposal?"

"It's an escape, madam, from the clutches of the law, the bloodhounds scenting your trail and coming down upon you."

She stared, dizzily. "I don't seem to have any other choice," she said.

TWENTY-FIVE

The constable was there, half a block away, pretending not to notice. Behind her was the step into the law offices. She was tempted to go back in, but that would give the game away. Instead, she decided on boldness. She walked slowly along Second, eyeing stores and windows. And at a cross street, she turned and was able to see Constable Roach, ambling along himself, staying a careful distance back, sometimes twirling his nightstick.

He was following. She didn't know what to do.

She tried another turn, another stretch of browsing. He meandered along behind.

Her path took her in the direction of the Drumlummon works, mine and mill, so that's the way she drifted. But the closer she came to the ramshackle structures and thundering mill, the more absurd was her direction. The roaring mill, belching smoke and fumes, throwing soot, leaving mucky pools of arsenic-laden waste, was not the place for a woman in a fine pink dress with a flowered hat to go.

She turned instead toward the mine, scarcely knowing what she would do there. But at least there was a supervisory structure, as rudely built as the rest. Everything at a mine was as temporary as could be managed. Mines all died. A sign, black paint on a white board, announced the Drumlummon. No gilt and plush here. The main shaft with its headframe and hoist lay ahead. At one side of it was a sorting yard. Waste rock was sent to the tailing heap; ore was sent to a trestle that carried it to the mill. But there was that other rude building, known as the dry room, where sweat-soaked miners coming off shift changed into dry clothing so they could walk to cabins or rooming houses comfortably. A changing room was crucial to the miners' health, especially in the depths of winter, where sweat-soaked clothing brought on pneumonia, and other lung diseases.

She glanced quickly behind her. The constable meandered along, ostensibly studying clouds, or whatever constables do.

She took her chance. It was not shift-changing time. She would not be likely to surprise some half-dressed men in there. There were, actually, two doors, though she didn't know why. She waited, aware that the constable was waiting, and then for a moment he was obscured by the corner of a trestle, and she plunged in.

She was surprised to see how rough it was. Whitewashed raw wood, benches, pegs to hang clothing, a few small windows for light. And miners' clothing, lots of it, hanging from pegs, there for the moment when it was needed. A potbellied stove was present for winter days, but was cold now.

But what to wear? Whose? And what would someone think to find his duds missing? And what would she do about her hair? Her dress, her hat? The inside of the cold potbellied stove would have to do. She rushed to a window, to see who or what was approaching. She didn't even see the constable, which worried her.

She flapped one set of britches after another, finally found some small ones, along with a small blue chambray shirt. And good luck, a dust cap. She hurried out of her dress, maddened by the small buttons, and got out of her chemise, and got the britches up, and got the shirt over her and buttoned, and was feeling some relief when the door opened, someone big and male looked around, scarcely noticing the small figure now in pants, and then the door closed. She pulled the dust cap over her hair and pushed the red strands upward under it as best she could.

She rolled up the dress, saddened that she could never wear it again, stuffed it into the potbellied stove, along with the hat with the silk flowers, and edged toward the door. But first she paused at a grimy window. She quickly decided to head for the headframe and lift. Below, Constable Roach was puzzling the disappearance of the woman in pink.

She walked straight into the lift, which she

shared with an empty ore car, and then she was dropping sickeningly, down into blackness, and finally to a halt some vast distance into the bowels of the earth.

The gate swung open, a rough man with a lamp shining from his hat yanked the ore car out, looked her over, and spat.

"You didn't bring the steels," he said. "Go back and get them."

She had been mistaken for a nipper, a boy who ran errands, brought supplies, such as new drilling steels. The gate slammed, the lift lowered, another ore car, full this time, was shoved in, and then she was catapulted upward, at a speed that dizzied her. After much rattling, she popped into daylight, and after a moment stepped out. She was glad to see blue sky.

She fled, but not without a stare or two from the surface men.

She saw no sign of Constable Roach, but that didn't dissolve her caution. She started down the grade, thought to retrieve her dress and hat from the stove, at least if she could carry it all with the pink hidden. She pushed into the dry room, found her things, rolled the dress into a ball she could cover with her white chemise, studied the hat, realized she would be fine if she could ditch its silk flowers, but she had trouble with it, and stuffed it into the stove. Then she fled the mine, sorry that she had stolen someone's shirt and pants. She didn't know what else she could do. Maybe she could return these, once she got into Kermit's britches. Yes, she'd do that. There must be mixups all the time in the dry room.

Constable Roach was nowhere in sight.

Only now did she realize she had been trembling. She had descended to the bottom of the mine. And that she never wanted to do again. It was like the portals of hell. She thought of those muckers who collected after each shift at Tip's saloon, and knew they were brave men.

She edged across open fields, reaching the washerwoman cabin in roundabout fashion, and was glad of its quiet welcome. For one more hour, one more day, it would grant her a safe corner of the world.

She changed out of the shirt and pants she had borrowed, garbing herself in Kermit's clothing, and then waited for dark. As usual, there was food quietly awaiting her, summer squash, split and baked and buttered. She thanked Tip, her shepherd. There had been a shift change at four, and now the second shift was hard at work. Someone went home in sweat-drenched clothing, and she was sorry. If things went well, the man would find his missing dry clothes in the morning.

Well into the eve, with darkness settled gently over Marysville, she ghosted her way through chill air to the Drumlummon, replaced the clothing on the same peg, and ghosted away. She had returned what was owed. That was important to her.

At her cottage, she pulled a blanket about her to ward off the chill. She did not dare light a fire. The day's events had rattled her. It was all fine that Hermes Apollo would begin a lawsuit, but he said it would take a year. Meanwhile, how could she survive? She had narrowly dodged Constable Roach this day. She had a haven, but only momen-tarily. She had food, but would Tip's crowd feed her month in and month out?

There comes a moment when the very impossibility of things becomes an inspiration. As she sat in that chair, swathed in whatever she could find against the bone-piercing chill, she arrived at that moment. In spite of the friendly help from Tip, and the peculiar support, for a price, of the lawyer, she was losing fast. She ought to escape. Maybe find work as a chambermaid in Butte, or maybe even hire out as a maid in a private residence. Bed and board. There were other, unsavory options, but she was damned if she would head that direction.

Whatever she did, she had nothing to lose.

The evening was young. She made sure she wore the darkest pants and shirt and sweater she had and ventured into the chill night. She thought of all the miners in their warm cabins, or in their warm saloons, or with their families around warm hearths, and she wanted nothing more than the warmth and comfort and security and freedom that they had.

The town was quiet. She walked past the Laidlow Funeral Home, noting the single lamp in its window. Her destination was the city building that housed the one-cell jail, Constable Roach's office, and a city hall. It was dark. The one-man police force was not there. She foun the door open, walked in, saw no one in the shadowed room, located a kerosene lamp, and lit it with a spark igniter that lay next to it.

Paper, pen, ink bottle, blotter. Ah, but what to write? A threat? No, bad idea. Something that would send the message. Yes.

> Constable Roach,
>   Eat, drink and be merry . . . and the rest of the proverb is in your hands.
> March McPhee

That was all. She penned another:

> Mr. Laidlow,
>   Eat, drink and be merry, before the eyes of the Territory are upon you.
> March McPhee

She left Roach's on his desk, and headed through the night to Laidlow's. The window lamp was extinguished. She remembered that the door was connected to bells, to alert the funeral home to the existence of a customer. She wondered whether she could manage to ease past it, decided she couldn't, walked around to the rear service door, found it open, left the message on a zinc-topped table, and escaped into the chill night.

She hoped the calling cards would stir up a little alarm.

Constable Roach would form a posse in the morning and head out.

She headed for the washerwoman cottage, wary of it, but it showed no signs of life. She crept in the back way, filled her carpetbag with her meager wardrobe, hid some squash and a melon in a cupboard, and headed into the bleak night. When she reached Tip's saloon she noted that it was shut, so she tried the alley door, and it creaked open. He had left it that way. She settled on the billiard table, and in spite of the hard surface, fell swiftly to sleep, in warmth, and with pretzels and water close at hand.

At dawn she was out, carefully closing the door behind her, and headed for the assayer's office. Mr. Wittgenstein had always been an early bird, in part because firing up his furnaces took a long while. It was just reaching daylight when she knocked and he opened.

"You, is it? I'm not surprised."

He motioned her in. It took only a few minutes to tell him her story, and he nodded.

"It's about what I supposed," he said.

"I need your help. It's a long wait before my case can be heard. And I'm being pursued. May I stay here during some nights, when you're away? When I need warmth and shelter. A refuge?"

"It's irregular," he said.

She agreed. "I'm a fugitive."

"They processed me at Ellis Island," he said. "Long lines, waiting to go through, and enter the land of the free. But now I am a citizen."

She didn't know where that was leading. "Well, thank you," she said.

"Ah, no! I am not done. Come here."

He led her to a small room boxed into a back corner of the building, and opened the door. A cot and chair rested there in the dim light of a small window drawing in the dawn light.

"I live out of town. Some nights I work late. Some days I wait for hours for my furnaces to do their job. Some nights it snows. I have this. It's yours when you need it. I have precious metals here, so I will give you a key. Always lock."

"Oh, sir!"

"There is another reason. I have watched this arrogant clan. They remind me of the old country. They bring me ore to assay. They're careless about what they say to each other. They were careless when they spoke of you and your mine, and how good it is, and how clever they were, figuring out how to get it and put you away for the rest of your life. They think assayers don't have ears. I hear more than most saloonkeeps. So . . . you see?"

"Oh, I am so indebted."

He stared. "No, it is a rare privilege to bring a little justice into the world. You see, I count my worth not by how much I make, but by how much I do to make this new land a better place." He smiled sadly. "I am an idealist. Don't ever be an idealist. It is a vice. It is better to be a poet."

She hugged him, but he was embarrassed and soon retreated to his furnaces. She put the carpetbag in the little haven, feeling as if the world was new.

TWENTY-SIX

Nothing happened. But March didn't expect to see newly sworn deputies collecting in front of the city building. Instead, she supposed the members of the clan would be in touch, seeking ways to hide their graft. Her next notes would alarm them further.

Now that she had refuges and means, she could work out a strategy, and that would be to start the Roaches and Laidlows to fighting one another, driven by fear of exposure. There was plenty to hide: a judge using his powers to steal property. A physician using his powers fraudulently to advance a theft of property. A constable doing the same. A funeral home inflating a bill as pretext to seize property. The Territory was lax, but not so lax that these things would be ignored. The trick was to set the clan against itself, if she could do it.

Late that afternoon, she slipped out of town, a wraith meandering along creek bottoms, unseen. She cut into the timbered flanks of the mountains, and made her way to the McPhee Mine, where from the safety of the dense forest she could observe the action. Now there was an armed guard, in fact Jerusalem Jones, and he carried a carbine. A work crew was industriously hauling out landslide rock her blast had loosened, one ore car after another, each load going into the tailings heap. It would not be long before the clan got her mine up and running. The crew was living in tents, hastily erected below the mine head. She saw wagons coming and leaving, bringing supplies up from Marysville.

The place would be well guarded all night, but she had a few other ideas. She retreated to her haven under the overhang, after watching it a while. Nothing was there. It was a good place to wait for dark. If they had found it, which she doubted, they had found nothing to suggest that anyone had been there in recent times.

Dark came faster with the change of seasons, and she was grateful. At dusk she climbed up the talus to the hollow in the cliff where she kept the blasting supplies, the place where she had a bundle of six sticks of DuPont, the bundle she decided not to use earlier. She added a fused cap.

When it was full dark, she made her way through the forest, carrying the fused dynamite. But she did not head for the mine, with its armed guards, not to the flat with the tents, but to a place well below, at the bottom of her mining claim where the steep road upward was flanked by a wall of decayed rock, great slabs of it that had weathered almost free from the mountain.

At a place where the road passed through a narrows, she peered about, wary of sentries, but there was only the quiet of the night and the deepening chill. She knew the exact place, but doubted she had the explosive she needed. She was working in starlight, but the big open sky of the West seemed to shed enough light for her to complete her task.

It was simple. Slide the charged bundle deep into the main fault that separated the weathered rock from the rest. First she felt about, hesitantly, wondering what might bite her. It might not be too late for snakes. But nothing did, and when she found the place that she thought would work best, she guided the dangerous bundle into the crack, slowly eased it back, halted when it bumped rock, and then she set it down. It would have to do. Her heart was pounding. The fuse did not extend all the way out, but that was fine. She could scratch the kitchen match there, the crack hiding its flame, and be out of there, a shadow upon the night.

She hoped it would work. If it did, it could bottle up the mine for many days.

She scratched the match. It flared. She touched the fuse, but it did not spark. She watched it until the match died, scratched another, and applied the flame. This time the fuse spat white sparks, the powder in it burning steadily. She withdrew, and headed downslope toward Long Gulch, and waited.

The flash and boom shattered the night. Some

shards of rock struck her, to her own shock. The percussion knocked her back. The boom echoed from surrounding slopes. The peace of the mountains stopped. She wanted to see, and waited a bit. She heard rattles and thumps, as the debris settled. Then she edged up the slope for a closer look. A great formless mass of rock had fallen across the mine road.

"That'll keep you from stealing my ore," she said to the night, and hastened away.

She did not hear shouts from above, which was good. They were probably just awakening to the reality that something had happened.

She walked back to Marysville, enjoying the bowl of stars above her, and the brisk night. She wondered what she would do next; it didn't really matter what. She would find the ways to drive the cabal out.

She slept away the last hours of the night at the washerwoman cabin, after first casing the place. She circled it, peered into the gloom, and finally entered. Nothing had changed. Constable Roach hadn't poked into this corner of his world recently.

She slept fitfully in the cold cottage, awakened, checked the view from the two windows and the laundry room, and then began planning her day. She knew what she wanted, to get her stolen mine back, and to throw every single crook in that cabal of kinfolk into the Territorial Prison at Deer Lodge. But it was one thing to have a goal;

another to get there. How could a one-woman assault on a powerful and politically entrenched gang succeed?

From somewhere she had this thought: a chain is only as strong as its weakest link. That was all she needed. She wondered where that old idea had come from, but it didn't matter. It seemed to reach her just when she needed it. The weakest link was the reckless young man, Jerusalem Jones, and his relative, Bum Carp. She didn't know how the pair were related to each other, much less the Laidlows, but they were. And they had been anointed to do the dirtywork, beginning with the fire that burnt her cabin.

Jerusalem Jones, the selfsame young braggart who bent an elbow in Tipperary Leary's pub. The selfsame loudmouth who regularly spilled the cabal's secrets to Tip.

She ate some uncooked corn off the cob, knowing she couldn't start a fire and boil it. She ground the kernels down, bit by bit, feeling like a milch cow. It was no way to live. She wore the shapeless green dress into Marysville, arriving early, and keeping a sharp eye for trouble. At Tip's saloon, she slipped to the alley and let herself in, and waited in the dusky barroom for the men she needed to talk to.

It took a long while, and not until nearly noon, when Tip opened, did he show up, entirely unsurprised to find her there.

"Does Jerusalem Jones still come in?"

"Sure, and he's noisier than ever."

"I'm hoping to set his alarm bells ringing."

"You are, are you?"

"Could you whisper in his ear?"

"Now, what would a proper man like me be doing that for?"

"I'm hoping you'll tell him you've heard some rumors."

"About?"

"What he did, and how the Territory knows everything."

"And if he asked where I got that, what shall I say?"

"Just smile, Tipperary."

"For you I'd do most everything, but brea trust. A man's business depends on trust, so I won't be telling Jerusalem a story. No, ma'am. That goes double for anyone running a pub."

"Well, tell him the truth then. Hermes Apollo's about to file a suit in the Butte district court against the whole gang. And the suit will name names and list what they've done. Every person in that clan will be named, including those who set fire to my cabin and killed my baby. And everything I've told you, it's happening. And now you've got the word."

"I'll buy him his third drink, and mention it," Tipperary said.

"You know something, Tip? You're a gem."

He stared at the back bar a moment. "You know, my bonny girl, the things a lad like me hears, they cut both ways. I'm glad you're here, and I'm glad we're putting down cards, because I've been listening, too. And it's not what you'd want to hear."

"Scots women are stronger than Scots men," she said.

"I don't know if you'd want to hear it," he said.

"If it's something I should know—"

He lifted a white hand with blue veins. "Himself, Jerusalem Jones, he has a wagging tongue of his own, once it's loosened a little. They're looking for you, and they'll find you. They know you're around. And here's the rub. They have no plans to send you back to Warm Springs, not after that convenient suicide note. You following? That lad Jones, he smiled, and he said, she'll meet her fate."

She sat, silently. He was talking about her own murder.

"If you'd like to go, my friends and me, we'll buy you fare to Butte. A woman can get good and lost in Butte, my bonny lady."

She wasn't ready to go to Butte. "We've traded threats, my life, the exposure of a corrupt clan. And you're the men with the ears."

"You're alive, March McPhee. There, I've said your name. You're a living woman, with a name to her, and it's not the name on some headstone.

We'll dip into the cookie jar, and we'll get you out, and we'll put you in good hands in Butte. We're an army in Butte. Please do that."

She was reluctant. "It'd leave an injustice staining the world."

He said nothing, wisely not pressuring her any further.

She watched motes of dust settle through a shaft of sunlight.

"You're looking after me," she said. "I don't know why. I might take you and your friends up on it, but not just yet. You see, things might happen fast. As soon as the lawyer files my case, it's out in the public, you know. It might take a long time to come to trial, but meanwhile there's these things out in the open. They can't afford to let them hang. Any reporter for any paper can have a look. Any official, he can have a look. Judge Roach. Constable Roach. You see?"

He smiled. "You're the bonny one, then. I knew it."

"If I live through the next few days," she said.

She eased out the alley door, studied the alley and deemed it safe, and made her way to Hermes Apollo's chambers, all the while keeping a sharp eye. Her nondescript green dress would not help her now. Nothing she wore would help her, if she were discovered.

The chamber, redolent of Havana cigars, with

flocked red wallpaper, always repelled her, and she knew the place was an expression of the tastes of her future husband, if it came to that.

He was pomading his slick hair, plastering it down, and ignoring her until it was just so.

"Is the suit ready?" she asked.

"Been ready for days," he said. "I simply haven't the time or energy to carry it to Butte. Travel costs money, and I'm certainly not getting any from you."

"Could I do it?"

He stopped messing with his hair. "You could, but won't."

"What's involved?"

"You hand it to the clerk of court, get a receipt and docket number, and leave my name and address."

"Then I could save you some time."

"No, you would deprive me of the pleasures of Butte. There are houses that welcome me with open arms, so to speak." He lipped his dead cigar. "Three houses and four exemplary ladies of the demimonde. If you'd only pay me, I could afford them all."

She absorbed that for a moment, and stormed out.

TWENTY-SEVEN

The bells at the door of the Laidlow Funeral Home clattered when she walked in at two in the morning, shattering the peace. A kerosene lamp burned quietly in the hall. She waited patiently in the quiet, hearing muffled thumps above, and finally the tread of feet down a stairwell.

Moments later Bum Carp appeared, bedraggled but clad in hastily drawn-up britches and the top of a union suit. His face lacked the attention of a straight-edge, and his dark hair tufted this way and that, an odd frame for his youthful face. He looked sleep-drugged, and indeed, was not entirely himself at that hour.

"Mr. Carp, I'm March McPhee," she said. "I understand you're Mr. Laidlow's relative."

"You need services, ma'am?"

"No, actually, I came to talk to you. I think it's time for a little visit. Have you a place where we can converse?"

"Here's good enough."

"It's customary to invite a customer to sit down, especially a grieving one," she said. "I've been grieving the loss of my boy, Fourth, we called him, because my husband was Kermit the Third. I do believe you know about that, don't you?"

He was rapidly wakening now, which was fine.

"Actually, I'm doing you a favor. I've come to warn you. I'll let you know privately what is going to be public soon, the exposure of your clan's rather unusual enterprises, Judge Roach's interesting decisions, Constable Roach's strange law enforcement, and of course your— What is he, uncle? Mortimer Laidlow's remarkable activities."

"What do you want?"

"I do believe that you and your cousin Jerusalem were at my husband's mine the night my cabin burned down and took my little boy, Fourth, with it. The Territory's about to learn all about that. Premeditated, you know, that's always worse. I think if you're smart, you'd put your shoes on right now and flee the Territory of Montana. People are talking, you know. You can't hide something like that for long, Bum Carp. Is that your real name, Bum? I doubt it. No parent would burden a boy with that."

"Who's talking?"

"By the time you find out, it'll be too late."

"This is all horse apples, isn't it? What's to keep me from hauling you over to the jail?"

"This hatpin, for starters, and more. Who's out there? In the dark. What's going to happen next? I've made my point, young man. Run when you can. It's all falling apart."

He glowered, not knowing what to do.

"Did you start that fire, Bum?"

"I was up at the mine."

"So Jerusalem did? The court papers say that both of you started it. You'll want to defend yourself when you testify."

He stared, plainly wondering whether to plow into her.

"Give me two dollars," she said.

"What? What?"

"You heard me. Go get it and give it to me."

"Two dollars?"

"I'm waiting."

Slowly, he turned, vanished up the dark stairwell, and returned, with two greenbacks.

"Place them on that table," she said.

He did. She picked them up.

"Good night, Bum," she said. "Go wake the constable and ask him about this, if you wish. It might comfort you—for now."

She opened the door, jangling the bells again, and stepped into clean night air. She left him standing there next to the kerosene lamp burning in a wall niche. He did not rush after her, and she hurried into the black, moonless night, her mission accomplished. It had been easier than she had thought it would.

He was not a born leader, she thought.

A round-trip ticket to Helena on the stub line to Marysville cost one dollar and twenty cents. She would have enough left over for a treat at the chocolate shop on Last Chance Gulch.

She boarded the morning freight, which had a coach attached, before the sun topped the mountain ridges to the east. There had been no one except a pair of drummers at the little station, and no one in the ticket window. The conductor would take her fare.

Maybe, in Helena, she could rattle the Roach clan a little more.

The wooden pews in the coach did not suggest first-class service, but the run was short, and her back could endure the half-hour of jarring. But she was in Helena while breakfast was still being served in the Territorial capital. She was early, but she had enough to enjoy a cup of coffee and a pastry in the Northern Pacific Beanery.

She wondered where she might find Jerrold Laidlow, MD. If indeed he was a medical doctor. She had her doubts. The only time she had seen him was in a cell of the county jail, where Judge Roach had thrust her, for alleged contempt of court. Helena was a bustling town; he could be anywhere, or nowhere.

But on Last Chance Gulch she spotted an apothecary shop, and thought that was as good a source as any. She entered a narrow dark room lined with large brown bottles and dark blue vials, and an egg-bald proprietor with a furrowed forehead.

"How may I relieve you?" he asked.

"Of what?"

"Pain, money, dyspepsia, what does it matter?"

"I am looking for a Doctor Jerrold Laidlow, and wish to be directed to his chambers."

He frowned, deepening those furrows. "Are you suicidal?"

"At the moment, inclined to homicidal."

"You will improve the human race," he said. "May I inquire what for? I can sell you more than he knows how to prescribe."

"You are suggesting his, well, mastery of medicine is limited?"

"Far be it from me to say anything of the sort, madam. But I hope you will investigate all options before placing your life in his hands."

"I must see him. He's a weak link."

"I've heard him called many things, but that's truly the best and most original." He brightened. "I was afraid that if I sent you to him, I'd be assuming some liability that I would rather avoid."

March liked this gent. "Well, I thought to improve his outlook by giving him advice, which is to leave the Territory while he can."

"Ah, indeed. In that case, I shall gladly supply his address. It's on Lawrence Street, west of the gulch, a frame house in which he has converted the parlor into his chambers. A sign advertises his business."

"Good, thank you."

"I have a favor to ask of you, madam. If you succeed, please tell me about it."

"I'll shake on it," she said.

She hastened down the gulch, found Lawrence, and turned up the street, climbing a steep hill. The run-down house was there, with a shingle advertising the doctor's wares, out front. She turned in, knocked, and got no response. She tried again, and this time Jerrold Laidlow himself, disheveled and grouchy, responded.

He looked her up and down. "Oh, I suppose so," he said, and let her in.

It took her only a moment to realize that the doctor was not entirely sober, and had not been sober for a long time. He led her into the parlor.

"Female problems, I presume," he said. "All right, prepare for the indignities."

"No, I've come to warn you about what's in your future," she said.

"I knew it. You're the Warm Springs suicide."

"Mad fantasies. Lunatic dreams. Now, let's just take one. Your demise. Let's say the highest officials in the Territory learn that you helped steal a gold mine? That you committed its owner to Warm Springs as a way to get rid of her? That you've already received the first payment, let me see, five hundred fifty dollars? Each of you with a full share in the stolen mine got that much, and those with half a share got two hundred seventy-five, and that was for the first month, with more payments stretching out for as long as the mine produces. Suppose that the Territorial governor sees the ledger, sees the names, sees how much boodle's been distributed, and who's getting it. Now suppose the officials learn that a certain Judge Roach and a certain undertaker in Marysville played a little game on the new widow, well, it'll all come out shortly. Of course not here in Helena, where the corrupt judge presides, but elsewhere, in another district. Now, another fantasy is that the two youngest of those in this cabal, the ones who deliberately set fire to the widow's cabin, and that fire took the life of her only child, let's suppose those two are scared of what's coming. Probably flee the Territory. If they don't they'll not only have to testify, they'll spend the next few years in the penitentiary. How's that for a mad fantasy, Doctor?"

"Sounds like fantasy to me. My decision to ship you to the asylum was right on the mark."

"Well, I'm not one to predict the future, Doctor, but simply to imagine it. Maybe reality will be different. Maybe this family cabal is so powerful that it's in cahoots with the Territorial officials. And nothing happens. In that case, the madwoman would be wrong, wouldn't she? Her vision of the future wouldn't resemble the real world, and real events, and real people. Then you could say you were right to ship her off to the lunatic asylum. Well, Doctor, what do you think?"

"You're buzzing about like a pesky horsefly. What's the drill? Are you threatening blackmail? Are you extorting me?"

She smiled. "It's out of my hands. I thought you'd appreciate the warning. By tomorrow you could be on a train to some safe place. Oregon, or South Dakota. Beyond the long arm of the law in this Territory."

"Extortion, that's what you're up to."

"Have I asked you for anything? Of course not. You seem to be having mad fantasies. Name my price. What am I demanding?"

"I'll learn soon enough," he said.

"I talked to an apothecary to find out where you live. Why does he think ill of you? Are you a real doctor?"

He nodded toward the wall. "There's my parchment."

"From a correspondence school?"

His gaze bored into her.

"What courses gave you the ability to judge my mind?"

He said nothing.

"The Territory will soon find out," she said. "The court will want to know the basis for your decision to send me to Warm Springs. Or was the basis a piece of my mine?"

"You certainly are a horsefly," he said, yawning.

"Enjoy your day," she said. "Now you have a reason to drink. Until now, you drank without a reason."

He laughed.

She headed into the morning, uncertain what had been accomplished. He was somehow tougher and sharper than she had imagined, and more dangerous. He was capable of wiring Constable Roach in Marysville to meet the next train, and capture her. In fact, the more she thought of it, the more she worried. She had overreached, and now there was new risk. The telegraph wires would pulse with urgent messages.

She remembered her previous trip in a caboose. But who could say what the next brakeman she encountered would do. The other option would be to wait a few days, until the constable got tired of meeting trains from Helena. But that wasn't an option, not with the few cents she had in her reticule. And now that the cabal was in trouble, Constable Roach would be on hand at every arrival, and probably departure, too.

The caboose seemed risky. But maybe a ride in a boxcar, or one destined for the Drumlummon, would work better. She hiked to the rail yards, waited several hours for the Marysville local to load passengers, and saw what she needed to see. A boxcar loaded with mining equipment. It wouldn't be comfortable, but the ride wouldn't last forever. From the far side, opposite the station platform, she climbed in, unladylike in her quick ascent, and found herself in a world of crates and barrels, along with a grizzled hobo.

TWENTY-EIGHT

The hobo took one look at her and pulled a knife from somewhere.

"Get outa here," he said, brandishing it.

She didn't argue. But no sooner had she moved toward the open door of the boxcar than a heavy jerk on the couplings threw her backward, and the train started to roll.

"I said get out. No women."

"Get out yourself," she snapped. She was tired of being hounded and bullied and robbed, entirely by males.

The train huffed and the wheels rolled.

The hobo's alert gaze altered slightly, but he kept the wicked knife in his hand.

"No women," he said again.

"Go find another car," she snapped.

The train was lumbering along now, swinging out of Helena. She was stuck with a tramp who looked ready to kill her and had a half hour to do the job.

"Get out. Find another car, or I'll knock you out of here," she said, wondering where that erupted from.

He didn't get out, but after a bit he slid the knife into a sheath hidden at his waist. His gaze never left her.

She knew somehow she was safe for the moment, but things might change at any time. The train was rattling along now, fifteen or twenty miles an hour; she could jump out, but it would kill her. Smoke and ash from the engine blew in, sooting her face.

"You're sitting on the wrong end of the car," he said. "Come to this end, and that stuff won't choke you."

"But you might."

"More than likely you'd choke me," he said, "and toss me out the door."

She laughed. She couldn't help it.

They sat facing each other for ten or fifteen minutes. She stared out the door, felt the ash and wind in her face, wondered if she could get outside of the car, climb one of those little ladders to its roof, and keep out of his sight. The reality was, she didn't even know where to step, or how to do any of it. And she saw nothing in the car that would serve as a weapon. Just big crates and casks of chemicals.

Still, the brief run was half over and she was still alive and unharmed.

Then he breached the silence.

"You broke or something?"

"No, I have a ticket to Marysville. It's very simple. There may be a man at the station I don't want to meet."

He grinned. "Copper, maybe?"

She didn't reply.

"You came to the right car," he said. "I know about coppers. Most are dumb as stumps."

"Why are you going to Marysville?" she asked.

He drew back into himself. "Got a job," he said.

"Mining?"

He laughed. "I'd no sooner go down into one of them pits than I'd walk into a church."

"I prefer sunlight—day and night," she said.

"Night's my time of day," he said.

"What kind of job do you have?" she asked.

The look on his face warned her she was getting onto dangerous turf.

That was the end of conversation. The train huffed up a grade, pushing deeper into the flanks of the Rockies, and then Marysville lay ahead.

"Don't get off at the station, even on the far side," he said. "Just wait. They'll run this up to the mine after dropping the passengers, and then you get off."

So he was helping her.

"There's a fat little bitch causing trouble around there," he said.

She felt insulted.

"I'm dealing with it," he added.

She no longer felt insulted.

The train hissed to a stop, its bell clanging, and down a way she saw people on the platform. The blue-clad constable was among them, as she had feared. She lowered her head until the crates hid her. The tramp eyed her carefully. But nothing happened, and in a moment, the train huffed and clanged its way to the Drumlummon, and wheezed to a halt. He smiled dourly at her and was out of the car the instant the train ground to a stop. She arose, looked around fearfully, but saw no one, and swiftly stepped down, using little strap-iron steps hanging from the car. She knew she must be a strange sight, a woman in that male world, but no one noticed, no one stayed her, and she drifted toward the road, and the Cruse house, and the washerwoman cottage.

It had been ransacked. A cupboard door was left open. She understood at once that the man-hunt would return again and again. They were looking hard now. No doubt some of those she had visited were talking, and now they knew for sure she was there, on the loose.

She was weary. There was no safe place. Food was scarce. Changes of clothing were in her carpetbag at the assay office, and there was still plenty of day left before she could get to it.

She headed out, skirting the aspen grove, edging the meadow, until she reached the Long Gulch road, and headed up it, wary of traffic. It would be a long time until dark, and the night would be cold, but her niche under the overhang near her mine might be a place of refuge. She encountered no traffic at all, and wondered about it. Near the road up to her mine, she cut into forest, working slowly through dense, cold woods. She paused at a place she knew would give her a look at her property, and discovered that the trail was still blocked by tons of rock. She continued upward, at points cutting toward her mining property, and when she finally viewed the mine, she found no one at work. The flat where her cabin had stood was empty of all habitation. There was nothing but ash save for a single tent. The mine was quiet. She wondered whether someone lay in the tent, threw a small rock at it, got no response, and edged closer. It was empty. There was not a mortal on the whole of her claim.

Was it because the mine lane was still blocked? Or because the charge she set in the mine shaft had sealed it beyond recovery? Warily, she walked the flat where her cabin had stood, looking for clues, and finding none. The tent was empty. She had hoped to find something warm, a jacket, a blanket, but it was no more than flapping canvas in chill mountain air. Cautiously, she walked up to the mine portal and peered in, edging up the grade, finding the wall of debris untouched. It was gloomy there, and she hastened out, debating whether to climb to her refuge upslope, or just use the tent overnight. It was eerie.

She studied the sky, and saw low gray clouds crawling over the peaks and ridges, pushing a haze before them, clawing down valleys. And above, a skin of white blotting the sun.

She could not stay there. What she hoped was a refuge could well kill her. She returned to the wall tent, unbuttoned its door, and wrapped it around her. It was not bad for a poncho, but she had miles to go to reach town.

The rain struck about when she reached Long Gulch, and rivered out of brooding gray clouds that sawed off the mountains. The cold shocked her. One moment she was making headway; the next moment arctic cold drenched her head. She pulled the tent door tight, suddenly aware that it was pure good fortune. The icy rain lashed her face, but at least most of it drained away, thanks to the canvas that she clutched tight. The rain turned to sleet, snapping at her head, her cheeks, her wrists. Winds rocked her, tried to tear the canvas off of her, and sometimes almost succeeded.

She was worn; this very day she had shared a boxcar with a violent tramp, discovered that her washerwoman haven had been ransacked, and now she had two miles of misery to reach town and blessed warmth.

She endured, step by step, even as the icy rain stole warmth from her and tried to undo the thin canvas armor that now preserved her very life. There could be no stopping now. Just pacing, no matter how tired, step by step, enduring whatever ice and rain and snow lashed her, caked her hair, numbed the hands that held the canvas to her chilled body.

I'm a Scot, she thought, and somehow that heartened her, though she doubted Scotland, girt by sea, could ever test her so ruthlessly. But somehow she endured, step by step, and finally, with the last of her energy, worked through the deserted streets of Marysville, found her key to the assayer's office, let herself in, and collapsed onto the floor, as water dripped away. The residual warmth of the furnaces lingered there like love, slowly easing the cold of her worn flesh.

The canvas lay on the floor, cold and soaked, leaving pools. But it had saved her life. The humble, tight-woven fabric had stayed the storm. She huddled around the still-hot furnace for a while, reviving, alone in the dark. Alive. She felt her way back to Wittgenstein's little hideaway in the corner, and found the welcoming cot. After a while, when the shaking had ceased, and the heat had lifted her spirits, she slipped into troubled sleep.

She knew nothing of the stormy night.

A tapping on the door awakened her all too soon.

"Forgive me, madam. Business hours approach."

She couldn't stay there by day.

"One minute," she said, springing out of the cot.

She found a dry dress, actually her shapeless Warm Springs one, got into it, jammed everything into the carpetbag, and opened.

"You were out in the storm," he said. "Here's this." He handed her the canvas, neatly folded.

He had started up the furnaces, and dawn was breaking. She must go.

"This place was the most welcome in my life," she said. "The rain caught me coming from my mine."

"Not much to see, was there?"

"Not a soul was there. I can't imagine it. I thought they'd be digging out."

He stared through the window at the dawning sky. "I'm going to do something I've never done—talk about someone else's assays. Your mine is probably dead. The ore pinched out in one lateral, is declining to a two-inch seam in the other, and not present at all on the face of the main shaft. The last batch of assay samples were, shall we say, the death rattle. The ore they brought in was so devoid of gold it wasn't worth mining. Four samples, and none of them promising. One had no metal at all. A pocket, exploited and gone."

She felt numb. "Nothing? All this for nothing? I'm a fugitive for nothing?"

He nodded. "They didn't bother to reopen the shaft."

"All for nothing," she said. "I've been running, homeless, for nothing."

He spoke softly. "And they've been hounding you for nothing, breaking every law for nothing."

She wanted desperately to lie down on the cot again. The world outside was cold and cruel.

"Are you well? If it's necessary, stay here for a while."

"I will go," she said.

He seemed ill at ease. She wanted to hug him, but instead, slipped out of the door, even as the half-light of the new day brightened. She hastened through empty streets, cleaned of manure by the rain, and found her way to Tipperary's saloon. As usual, the alley door was open, and she entered the cold dark confines, suddenly desperate for food. She plucked up two pretzels from the jar, settled on top of the billiard table, and tried to process what all this meant. What was she fighting for now? What could she expect? Why was she here? Where could she go? She didn't know, but she couldn't shake the idea that her troubles were worse than ever. She didn't know why, only that the Roach cabal wanted to catch and silence her worse than ever before.

TWENTY-NINE

March heard the thump of feet, the sound of people running, muffled shouts, a clatter of wagon wheels, and whistles. She lay on Tipperary's billiard table, desperately trying to make sense of anything, and no more rested than when she fell into the assayer's cot.

Something was amiss. Fear lanced her; there were men here who wanted badly to return her to Warm Springs. She crept to the fogged window, peered out, and saw men hastening, all heading one direction. And just vanishing from her view was the Laidlow ebony hearse. Death, then.

She weighed the consequences of stepping outside. She sensed this was something she needed to know about, but couldn't say why. She wore only the shapeless dress of the institution she had fled, but maybe that was good. She didn't wish to attract attention. It would not be like wearing a pink dress and a straw hat laden with silk flowers. On a peg she found a cape, something some customer had left behind, and now she borrowed it, wrapped herself tightly, eased out the alley door, past the odorous outhouse, and up the empty alley.

Ahead, all noise had vanished and there was only a strange, oppressive silence. She walked steadily toward Second Street, her chest tight with fear. But no one stayed her, and then she reached the cross street and beheld the crowd, several hundred strong, crowded about the law chambers of Hermes Apollo. Something terrible was happening. The hearse stood there, and at the door stood Constable Roach, a brown folder clutched under his arm. Suddenly she understood what that folder contained, understood what this was about, and felt terror course through her. She chose to stop there, at the edge of the alley, even if the distance kept her from seeing everything. The awful thing was that she already knew.

The crowd kept expanding. It looked like most of the males of Marysville were collecting in front of the law office. Constable Roach stood on the front step, watching the crowd quietly. He seemed a model of calm. Apart from whispering, that occasionally hissed in the breeze, this army of males was silent.

Someone from Laidlow Funeral Home was pressuring people away from the black drays that stood, tails switching, in black harness. She studied these men, thought she spotted Tipperary, but at that distance was not sure. Finally, Laidlow's two flunkies edged out the door, carrying a stretcher, and eased through the gawkers, with Laidlow himself pushing men out of the way.

March got only a glimpse, when the pall was

being carried out the door of the law office. On it lay Hermes Apollo, his white shirt and dark waistcoat bloodied, streaked with red, long, cruel cuts. He had been knifed. He had perished from multiple stabs and slices and gouges. His reddened arms flopped over the pall, even as Jerusalem Jones and Bum Carp pushed their way through the gawkers to the ebony hearse, and pushed the late lawyer inside.

Oh, Hermes, she thought. Oh, Hermes. Because of me.

"A fiendish murder," Constable Roach said. "I will pursue the killer to the ends of the earth, down into hell if I must. Now be gone. Let the streets be safe again."

But no one moved. Laidlow conferred with Roach on the steps, each of them carrying folders stuffed with paper, and then he walked through the horrified crowd, climbed up on the hearse, took the lines, and gently slapped croups, urging the black horses through the spectators, who continued to watch in deep silence.

March knew what was in those folders.

And knew she would be next.

And felt a powerful arm wrap her, a hand across her mouth preventing a scream, and then the prick of a knife in her side.

"They want a suicide," the tramp said. "Fits the note you left."

She writhed, struggled, briefly pulled him out

from the alley into the view of the others, who were all watching the hearse wind its way to the funeral home. But no one saw, and no one came.

He force-walked her ahead of him, expertly pressuring her in ways that made the steps seem almost routine. But the slightest resistance brought the blade into her side, so she felt its sting, its heat, and its terror.

She searched for help, both wanting it and knowing that if it arrived, that blade would sink deep into her. No help came.

"Too bad I didn't peg you in the boxcar," he said. "Wrong description. But it don't matter now. Where do you want to commit suicide?"

She kept silent. They walked further. Her limbs ached from the pressure.

"My mine," she said. "It's two miles out."

She would live that long, anyway.

"Two miles out? Fat chance."

"It's where I lost my husband. My baby boy. And the mine."

"You'll croak in a boxcar. That'll do fine. I'm going to let go of you. Walk in front of me. Don't run, don't try nothing. I'm a lot faster than you."

She felt herself freed, and it was all she could do not to run. She turned abruptly.

"Where?" he asked.

"My mine."

He yanked her violently and steered her toward the rail siding that ended at the Drumlummon at the edge of town. A man on the street stared.

"I'm going to my home," she said, and veered again, and again she was yanked violently and now cakewalked directly toward the rails. Her heart was hammering. She walked faster and he was right behind. She saw a string of flatcars but no boxcar. Not one.

"Sonofabitch," he said.

"My mine," she said. She turned abruptly, started up Third Street, walked straight through town, past people now, the tramp one step behind, muttering. She speeded up; he speeded up. She swerved; he swerved and caught her, his iron grip instantly crushing her shoulder. She felt the prick of steel in her side, and stopped at once.

"Walk slow and easy," he said. "You're dead if you mess around."

"Then I have nothing to lose," she said.

Tipperary was walking beside, white apron, axe handle in hand. He passed forward of her, paying no attention. One of his patrons, dust cap and all, was coming up fast.

Her every instinct was to break loose and run. Instead, she halted abruptly, and the tramp slammed into her, unbalanced, and she twisted right.

The thud of the axe handle hitting the tramp's head, and then a groan, was all she heard. She landed on the clay street. Another thud, some cursing, and yells. She crawled up, turned around, found the tramp sprawled in the road.

"Be you safe?" he asked.

She felt her side, and the stickiness there, but it was nothing. "Think so."

Now men flooded in, mostly gawking.

The tramp groaned. Someone collected a long, bloody knife with a narrow blade.

"Killed the lawyer," someone said.

"You're bleeding, Miss."

She was. "I'll put a plaster on," she said.

"What's this?" someone asked.

"It's him that killed the lawyer and tried for her. And we're not done, not yet," Tip said.

"I don't follow you."

"It was hired, and we'll go for them."

She was handed a rag, and she pressed it to her side, and it reddened. She felt dizzy.

"Who's this woman?"

"March McPhee, she whose mine was stolen, whose boy was killed."

"You're her are you? I thought you were a madwoman."

"And her freedom was stolen, too," Tip said. "A good place to shut away a woman whose mine they took from her."

"And what's all this? A tramp loose on the streets, Leary?"

"It's silence they were buying, right when they were about to be exposed, the whole bloody lot of them. You'll see it come together soon enough. We need men. Come along to the constable."

She knew some of them now. They were Tip's customers, but there were others. Her side smarted, but there wasn't much of any blood.

"Mrs. McPhee, wait safe in my place of business, and put a little spirits on your cut."

"Later," she said. "I will come along."

"There's a Celt," Tip said. "Lift him up now, and carry him."

The tramp had a bloody lump on his skull, and his breath was rasping. His fingers clutched and unclutched the knife that was no longer there. He opened his eyes, closed them, and went limp again. Two men in dust caps lifted him awkwardly.

March felt faint. But she was not going to miss any of it.

"What's this? What's this?" yelled Constable Roach, pushing his way through the crowd. There he was, natty blue uniform immaculate, mustachios trimmed to the last hair.

"Here's the killer, and he tried for her," someone said. "See, here's the bloody knife, and it's the lawyer's own on it."

"The madwoman," Roach said. "Got her. She's behind this."

"Constable, hand me that billy club," Tipperary Leary said.

"What are you talking about? I'm taking you in."

Tip's axe handle cracked down on the constable's hand. He howled.

"You getting us into a jackpot, Leary?" a man asked.

"He hired it done; him and his clan. Laidlow's one. It'll come clear. Check the constable, see he's clean, and bring him."

"You'll pay for this; twenty years in Deer Lodge," Roach said.

"You won't live to see it, because you and this here tramp, and a few more, you'll see the noose and nothing after."

The constable's face drained of color.

"Bring him along," said Tip.

Hesitantly, the crowd caught Roach.

"You'll pay, you'll pay," Roach said. "You'll pay the price, and do time. Get your hands off me. I'm a peace officer."

The crowd hesitated.

"Guess I'll haul you there myself," Tip said, and began marching the constable toward the village lockup. Uneasily, the rest followed, two of them carrying the tramp. It was an uneasy, uncertain bunch that dragged the tramp and the constable straight through town, catching stares and glares at every hand, from every storefront. This was something unheard of in quiet Marysville.

Strangely, as they passed the assay office, Wittgenstein joined them, wearing his thick canvas apron. "Are you well, Mrs. McPhee? Do you need help?"

"I'm getting help from the truest men in town."

They reached the city building, with its little lockup. The constable's office was orderly. She looked in vain for the brown folders, the papers that Hermes Apollo was about to file, and saw nothing. That shot fear through her.

"There's never a paper on the man's desk, Mrs. McPhee," Tip said. "We'll look in a minute. He directed the men carrying the tramp to settle the man in the cell, and then the constable.

"Check him for a key," he said.

They found a ring of keys on the constable, and nothing more, and pushed him in.

"Are you sure you know what's what, Leary?" A town merchant named Spreckels was objecting.

Tip circled behind the constable's desk, opened desk drawers, found some brown pasteboard folders and pulled them out. Written on one was *McPhee vs Laidlow, Roach, et al.*

"The lot of them, this shadowy clan, all kin one way or other, was about to be exposed. The lady and her attorney, God bless his soul, were going to file papers in Butte, since Judge Roach in Helena's a part of it all. The complaint's here. The McPhee Mine, it's gone, a pocket is all, but this lawsuit had to be stopped, and they tried."

"Oh, horsepucky, Leary," another merchant said. "Have you lost your mind?"

"There's the tramp's knife, and it's bloody to the hilt," Tip said. "And who was paying him to protect their reputations?"

The crowd jammed into the little office seemed uncertain, divided, and fearful.

Then Mortimer Laidlow burst in, armed with a shotgun. Jerusalem Jones and Bum Carp followed, with drawn revolvers. The crowd edged back, isolating Tip Leary and March McPhee at the desk.

"Heard it was like this," the undertaker said. "We've come to restore law and order."

THIRTY

Oddly, nothing happened. The undertaker crouched at the door, shotgun in hand, backed by two nephews, revolvers in hand. Over in the jail, the tramp was coming around, shaking his head. Constable Roach stared. Behind the desk, folders in hand, Tip Leary stood, and beside him, March. And a dozen other citizens stood about, paralyzed.

It could turn into bloody mayhem. March planned to hit the floor. If she lived.

Constable Roach spoke quietly:

"Mr. Leary, release me. You are holding the key. Mortimer, lower that shotgun. You might hurt someone. You young men, holster your revolvers. The rest of you, stand quietly."

Tip paused only long enough to see whether Laidlow would comply instead of firing, saw that the undertaker was reluctantly lowering his weapon a few inches so the barrel pointed at ankles rather than faces and chests, carefully unlocked the cell, let the constable out, and closed it again, keeping the tramp within. The lock snapped hard.

Constable Roach stepped toward his desk. There were tears in his eyes. He was as natty as ever, not a speck of dirt on his blue uniform, neatly shaven, his mustache trimmed, his gaze observant. But his lip twitched. It was one thing he could not control.

"Mortimer, the shotgun, please."

There was a strange aura about the constable. He was without weapons, yet at that moment the most commanding mortal present, a Moses carrying the Ten Commandments.

Reluctantly, the undertaker surrendered the weapon. The constable did not heft it or point it; instead, he placed it on his desk.

"Boys, unbuckle your belts, and hand me the revolvers in their holsters."

Slowly they did. They handed him the belts. Jerusalem was glaring, and the glare announced that he was being betrayed.

March marveled. The constable was disarming men on the very edge of madness.

"Is anyone else armed?" the constable asked.

No one was, except for Tip's axe handle, which Roach saw and ignored. Tip simply tucked it in his arms.

"Very well. We'll try not to keep Mr. Laidlow busy. You wonder about me now. I have been struck by lightning," the constable said. "Put it this way. I'm a copper, sworn to keep peace and order. I wasn't keeping my oath of office until just now. But we sometimes receive guidance. Who knows what and when and where? Or maybe it's just conscience. I am not who I thought

I was. It's a revelation. While I did not commission various crimes, I have known of them and did not object to them, and share the guilt of them. I should not be wearing this uniform."

He held out his hand to Tip. "The keys, please."

Tip handed Roach the jail keys. Roach headed for the iron-barred jail door, and flipped the lock once again.

"Mortimer, you and the boys walk into that cell."

"But, Thomas," the undertaker said. "This is all nonsense."

Roach said nothing, a quiet pillar of blue, and such was his power, even unarmed, that the three meekly entered, joining the tramp. March could not imagine what powers the constable had that would achieve these things.

Roach swung the squeaking iron door shut and locked it.

He turned to the rest. "We'll restore order here first. Then we will see to justice. I am part of a clan of people who overreached, and ended up commissioning murder to keep our secrets from the world. When I've restored civil order and achieved justice for the victims of our crimes, I will turn myself in. My testimony will convict me. But first I will report to authorities in Helena what has happened and why it happened, and set justice on its way."

He turned to March.

"Madam, we owe you more than an apology. It is upon us to make things right."

She listened, amazed, and nodded.

"First we stole your mine, conniving at law and through violence to take it away at the dawn of your widowhood; then your son was lost to a fire these two boys set, intending to drive you away forever. Gold inspired all that. Gold is what loosened every shred of conscience. Then to silence you, we had you declared mad by our very own quack and put you away forever. And it turns out, that was only the start. When we discovered you got free and were preparing to go to law, we realized even filing the suit would expose the whole clan, so my cousin, Judge Roach, made certain arrangements in Helena, and another death happened, and yours would have followed."

Those who did not know the story stood, mesmerized. There was only dead silence in that small office.

"It is not enough to apologize. But before I'm done, I will do all in my power to restore you to your life, liberty, and possessions, and bring an end to my clan's abuse of government power. And then they'll put me away."

The dignified man stood rigid, and she saw his eyes were wet.

She supposed she should say something, acknowledge something good, or thank him for something, but all she could manage was a nod.

He might make good for some things, but he had a part in the loss of her son. And the brutal death of her attorney. She nodded.

He addressed the crowd. "You may stay or go. You may witness the things I will do next. You may watch me deal with brothers and cousins and nephews. You may watch me deal with myself. And you may follow me to Helena, where I will bring the matter to Territorial officials. What I do now, I do in a fishbowl."

March chose to leave. She wanted desperately to walk the streets of Marysville freely, not as a hunted woman, not as a reputed madwoman on the loose. She walked quietly past staring eyes, some of them friendly eyes, eyes rimmed with sympathy, and out onto the unpaved street where chill mountain air rolled down the slopes.

She was far across the sea from Scotland. Her Kermit lay buried nearby. Her dreams had vanished, every one. Her dear boy was ash. The future was a blank.

Tip joined her. "Would you like some company, March?"

"Always, Tip," she said.

Center Point Large Print
600 Brooks Road / PO Box 1
Thorndike, ME 04986-0001 USA

(207) 568-3717

US & Canada:
1 800 929-9108
www.centerpointlargeprint.com